# Faces in the Moon

*A Novel*

## By Betty Louise Bell

UNIVERSITY OF OKLAHOMA PRESS

NORMAN

**Library of Congress Cataloging-in-Publication Data**

Bell, Betty Louise, 1949–
  Faces in the moon / by Betty Louise Bell.
     p.  cm. —(American Indian literature and critical studies
series ; v. 9)
  ISBN-13: 978-0-8061-2601-2
  ISBN-10: 0-8061-2601-9
  1. Indian women—United States—Fiction.  2. Indians of
North America—Fiction.  I. Title.  II. Series.
PS3558.E4857F3   1994
813'.54—dc20                        93–42498
                                         CIP

*Faces in the Moon* is Volume 9 in the American Indian Literature
and Critical Studies Series.

The paper in this book meets the guidelines for permanence
and durability of the Committee on Production Guidelines for
Book Longevity of the Council on Library Resources, Inc. ∞

5  6  7  8  9  10

*To Lizzie Bell and Edward Andrew McClanahan,*
*for stories past and stories to come*

*I like simple relationships.*

*Yes.*

*Uncomplicated people.*

*Yes.*

*Don't you get tired of histories and explanations? There should be definitions for good and bad. If someone does something bad, it should be just bad. No histories.*

*Then we would have no literature.*

(from a conversation with Barbara Johnson)


*We make art out of our loss.*

Linda Hogan

*Faces in the Moon*

*Raising voices*

I WAS RAISED on the voices of women. Indian women. The kitchen table was first a place of remembering, a place where women came and drew their lives from each other. The table was covered with an oilcloth in a floral pattern, large pink and red roses, the edges of the petals rubbed away by elbows.

I remember now.

They spent their lives telling stories. The same stories, sitting in the same places, giving the same answers, warning children with a shake of the head and the tease of memory. Always finding, in the beginning or summing up, a detail undiscovered or a cruel motive revealed. In this way the stories lived, never finishing in circumstance or death. Or even in the storyteller herself.

I listen. My contribution to the story was to pretend innocence and listen, my eyes and mouth wide. "Shut your mouth, it gonna freeze that a way," my mother said from across the table. I pressed my lips tight and listened with my eyes, watching for a new detail in the turn of a mood, listening for the story in my mother's face.

4

I grew tired of living in the past and craved to find my stories in narratives of direction and purpose. I lived in the time of choice, where a person has only to believe to make it true. I have lived in desire these four decades and practiced invention for just as long, but no matter how great my desire to run away from home, to live in a place and history free from secrets, I always take up my position at the table, in the early morning hours, and listen for those women's voices.

*Dust, outlaws, pretty black-eyed Indian women raising children alone, chopping their way through cotton, good-ol' boys and no-good men. Full-bloodied grandmothers, mixedblood renegades and lost generations, whirling across the red earth in forty-nine Chevys, drunk on homemade beer, and aged by years of craving under the hot Oklahoma sun.*

When I'm fast, skillful and ready, I almost outrun them. But in the long distance they pass me, each running faster than I could have guessed. I hear my great aunt Lizzie cluck, "Sister, y'all can put lipstick on a hog but it's still a pig."

And I know their stories have grounded my sympathies, speaking through my spirit without time or place or will, Momma, Auney, Lizzie: they come alone or together, sometimes carrying with them Uncle Jerry and Uncle Henry and Robert Henry. Sometimes, they simply stand in the mortal light of their beloved Hellen, Lizzie's sister-in-law, Momma's mother, my grandmother. But, always, their real companion is Lucie, the child who sat and listened and stared into their stories, the child whose place I have taken.

The last time I saw her, she was running down the hills of southern Oklahoma and screaming at the top of her lungs, "I am Quanah Parker!" I have tried to find her, I have tried to know her but, as I sit here at the kitchen table, she comes only in their voices.

On clear full nights, I have seen Grandma's or Lizzie's face in the moon. Sometimes, my mother's face floats across it. If I'm lucky, I can make out Lucie, squinting down at me and waiting, like a patient memory, for my claim.

*Beat the drum slowly . . .*
*don't . . . stop . . . too . . . fast*

"YOUR GRANDMA was a full-blooded Cherokee," my mother said again and again, as far as I can remember. It was the beginning of a story, the beginning of a confidence, and I lean forward, knowing that in the next few minutes no cheek will be pinched, no broom handle swung, no screams or tears wasted. I listen and watch, grateful to be part of the circle. Her words come slow, a chant filling her sunken face and smoothing her wrinkles. Across the kitchen table, I never take my eyes off her.

I did not hate her, then. It was easy to believe in the photograph on Lizzie's bureau: a dark-eyed beauty with olive skin and black hair to her waist, shapely in a cotton housedress and holding a newborn baby. She stood forward in a new field, the baby close to her cheek, the woods far behind her. As a child I called the woman "Momma," slipping close to the photograph and tracing her outline with my fingers, whenever I passed through Lizzie's parlor. After my great aunt's death, it was harder and harder to put the pretty girl with the child together with the fat, beat-up woman who cursed and drank, pushed into her only threat, "Maybe I'll just run away and leave y'all to yourself."

Some tension had given, some spirit snapped in the space of ten years, and the pretty girl had swollen into fatigue and repetition. In her last years a big cozy mother appeared, in short housedresses with snaps down the front and letters sticking out of her pockets, letters written to me on scraps of paper, backs of envelopes, and carried around for weeks, even months, before she dropped them in the mail. Her running scrawl refused time, pushing ahead of it the events of her day and health, always confessing her secret love and pride in me, and arriving months after the fact.

But, long before the letters began to arrive, long before she knew she had something to say, she had already lost me to her stories. And there, I loved and forgave her.

"You was always her favorite. She was crazy 'bout you. I never seen her take to nobody the way she took to you. Ain't that right, Rozella? She was always too good for the likes a us. Uppity Indian. Her nose so turned up, her own shit don't stink."

"What did she look like?" I ask.

9

"Don't y'all member Lizzie?"

I shrug, my palms turned wide and open. I remember but I'm not supposed to remember. And I want to hear it again. I listen for Lizzie's name, watching as she moves before me in a calico apron and a tight face. She never smiles. Even as Momma and Auney move from laughter to tears, Lizzie stands silent and unamused.

"She was an Indian," Momma says. "She looked a lot like our momma, the same black hair and black eyes."

"Like us?"

"Y'all carry the Indian blood, that's for sure. Your black hair and Rozella's quiet ways, ain't no mistaking y'all. I ended up with the Scotch blood. Don't look like there were a drop left for y'all. Member that woman ask me if I'm Irish? Black Irish, she says. I'm a thinkin she means nigger, and I almost give her a beating right in front of the chicken shack. I just look her in the eye and say, as cool as you please, 'There ain't no nigger in my woodpile.' But Lizzie and momma, they looked Indian."

"Indian," Auney says with a nod and a blow of smoke.

She was my spinster aunt, a survivor of four

marriages, and my mother's chorus since birth. When one of her marriages broke up or she was looking for a new start, she came to us. And there, she was my mother's constant companion and an angel to me: silent and placid, she told no tales and didn't hit. And she gave me everything, except her bingo money. She drank and married hard-drinking no-good men. They almost killed her, more than once, but the closest she came to fighting back was to refuse to forget.

"I can forgive," she explained, "but I can't forget."

When she had had enough she came to us, put on her hairnet and went to work in the cafeteria with my mother, giving her slow attention to portions of corn and mashed potatoes. She never bothered with divorce, she simply lived in one married name until the opportunity for another came along. And like my mother, she just as easily switched from married to maiden name without consistency or legal considerations.

They were Evers, sometimes more, sometimes less, but always Evers. The daughters of Helen Evers and some no-account traveling Scotch preacher who never married their mother, turning up only to impregnate her a second time, and leaving them, finally, on the side of the road. The young Indian mother walked, carrying one baby and coaxing the other, until she came to a junkyard. There, she made a home for them in an abandoned car. There, until the rent money was saved, she left Gracie in the back seat to look after the baby, Rozella, while she walked into town and looked for work.

"You member, Rozella," my mother's mind fluttering from one story to the next, "the time I locked you in the outhouse?"

"I member."

Momma lit her cigarette from Auney's and spoke to me. "Your grandma used to have to go to work in town. Five miles there and back, she walked. Ever day, even Sundays. She was afraid someone would steal us, so she always locked us up in the house." Her eyes darted across mine, and she blushed with shame. "It was just an old shack, tar paper and cold in the winter."

"Cold."

"We was always up to no good." Her face lit up. "Still are, eh Rozella?"

"Yep. Sure was. Your momma was always the ringleader."

My mother took the compliment with a laugh.

"As soon as your grandma was down the road, we scrambled right out the window and back 'fore she got home that night. More coffee, Rozella?"

Auney was a strong coffee drinker. She'd been waiting for the offer for some time but instead of saying "yes," she looked down into her empty cup, took a drag on her cigarette, and came as close as she allowed herself to expressing want. "I believe so," she said in a slow and uncommitted drawl. She lived with us, on and off, for most of her life, but she never asked nor took without multiple invitations and assurances of plenty. That, my mother said, was the Indian in her.

Momma brought a new cup and the coffeepot to the table. She filled their cups and poured me half a cup. I wanted to smoke too but knew better than to ask.

"One day, you member Rozella?"

"I member."

"You went to the bathroom and I locked the door from the outside." Momma laughed, Auney blushed. "You didn't so much as raise a yell. I heard you try to open the door. But then you got real quiet."

"How did Auney get out?" I was the audience, and I held the story's cues.

"She did the durnest thing. I'm waiting out

13

front, wandering when she's gonna start yelling, and here she comes around the corner of that outhouse. What a sight you was, Rozella. I thought I was seeing things when you come around that corner." Momma turned to me. "She was covered with shit and piss from head to toe. She crawled right out of that damn hole! And she stunk! Lord have mercy."

"Amen."

"Momma came home that night and whupped the living daylights out of me. She whupped Rozella too."

"She did. Yes, she did."

"She said the county'd come and get us if we didn't behave. They woulda, too. A young Indian woman with two little girls and no man around."

"No man."

"But she kept us together. I wander how she did it, Rozella?" The kitchen curtain flapped. Momma went to close the window and found it shut tight. "Witches, Rozella. You member them witches down there in old man Jeeter's river?"

"Sh-h-h," Auney said. "Y'all gotta watch who y'all call up."

Momma laughed and turned to me. "Your Auney were always afeared a them witches. Long

14

afore our momma died, she'd a shiver and shake anytime she come near that water."

"Now, Grace, I weren't the onliest one afeared."

"That's true," Momma admitted, "true enough. Momma used to say only fools don't know what to be afeared of. And the good Lord save us from them. Eh, Rozella?"

"Ain't nothing scarier'n fool. The God's truth."

*In the dream I'm being chased. Through city streets, down alleys, only a few slippery feet ahead of the monster behind me. I feel his reaching darkness, gaining and gaining, almost in grabbing distance. I watch the horror of running without moving, screaming without noise, the terror striking and missing, striking and missing, and I pull myself treading to the surface. Sweating and shaking, I lie still in my corner of the room. "Shoo," I whisper, "Go on."*

"Those was tough times," Momma said. "The Depression and the wind blowing the topsoil clean outta Oklahoma. Times was rough all over. There was no welfare, no nothing for an Indian woman with two little girls to feed. Even ifn there was, she had that Indian pride, don't take nothing from nobody."

"Member she beat me fer askin Mz. Wilkins for that apple?"

15

"I thought she was gonna kill you."

"Almost did."

"Why'd Grandma do that? It was just a apple." The words slipped out of my mouth. I knew better. "I mean," I tried to explain as I watched the humor drain from Momma's face, "why'd she have to be so mean?"

"What ya know 'bout it? It ain't ever just a apple. Things ain't never that simple. 'Cept you, sometime." Auney dropped her laughing eyes, and Momma commenced shaking her finger at me. "Missy, ya ain't but ten years old and you think ya know it all. Ya'll don't know donkey shit."

"I know something," I mumbled and pushed my shoulders back.

"Horse manure."

Auney laughed and gagged on her smoke. Through a fit of coughing she tried to say, "Grace . . . we . . . was . . . the same way."

"At her age Momma was dead and we was on our own with that old devil Jeeter. We had to grow up fast, it ain't the same."

I considered the distance from my mother across the table and gambled, "I can take care of myself."

"I wisht I believed it. I'd a take the first greyhound bus and leave youse to yourself. The trouble with you, Missy, is you ain't never knowed hard

16

times. Ya don't know what it means to spend just as much time *not* looking hungry as being hungry." She was wrong, but I knew better than to gamble again. "I wisht I'd a had a mother to look after me. Maybe things a been different for me."

"Ya did your best, Grace."

"Lord knows I tried. I'd tried and tried till I'm a plumb tired out from trying."

"Plumb tired out."

"I tried to forget an' go on living. But those was hard times. Don't seem like there's a way a forgetting 'em. I member Momma like it was yesterday. I see her as clear as I see myself. I member her taking off down that road ever morning, walking those five miles to town to clean the Wilkins house and the Davis house . . ."

"And that one with the big white porch. The Johnson house."

"Yep. Those white women worked her to death, and the white men was always touching her up. Sometimes she'd come home crying. You member, Rozella?"

"I member."

"You member how we used to sit on old man Jeeter's back porch and watch for her in the moon?"

"I member."

"The day she died she said she'd be watching for us from the moon. You member?"

"I member."

"Used to be we'd see her. Most every night. All's we had to do was sit on old man Jeeter's back porch and watch for her. Soon those eyes a hers would be looking at us."

"Yep. Plain as day."

"We sit right there and talk to her like she could hear us. About old man Jeeter and the hard life we had without her." Momma laughed and shrugged. "Those eyes a hers would change. Look like she were going to kill somebody."

"You member, Grace, what she used to tell us?" Momma and Auney laughed, and I saw Lizzie turn from her work at the sink and almost smile.

"I sure do." Momma leaned toward me, as if I hadn't heard it a hundred times before, and said slowly, "Don't mess with Indian women."

"Less you're a fool."

"Even a fool got more sense 'n that."

"Grace, you ever see Momma after ya left old man Jeeter's place?"

"Used to be when I ran away with that old man Baptist preacher, I'd see her. Now and again. You see her, Rozella?"

"Now and again."

Momma waited for Auney's words to clear the room. We waited for what Auney would not say. Then Momma laughed and said, "Used to be we believed Indians went to the moon when they passed on." The joke passed through Momma's face before she spoke. "What y'all think? We gonna make it to the moon?"

"I can't see why not."

"Me too?"

Momma lit a cigarette. Auney said low and careful, "I believe so."

"You just tell them you're Hellen Ever's grandbaby. She ain't gonna let them turn ya away. They'd have a fight on their hands, sure enough. Wouldn't knowed what hit 'em. Ya member, Rozella?"

"I member."

"I remember."

Momma laughs, Auney stops mid-draw on her cigarette. "You weren't even born. How can you member?"

"I do remember."

My mother looks at me. The kitchen curtain flaps above my head. Finally, she says, "You musta dreamt it."

"Dreamt it."

19

*In the hour of the wolf . . .*

SOME PARENTS believe children have no memories. They hold their stories and lives until they are ready to return them, with full chronology and interpretation. History is written in this complicity, an infinite regression of children forgetting and remembering. It takes a long time to remember, it takes generations, sometimes nations, to make a story. And sometimes it takes a call in the night before the story is known.

Now, a lifetime later, when the phone rang at four in the morning, I pulled myself out of a strong sleep, knowing the voice over the phone before I heard it.

"How're you, Mabel? How's the girls and the grandkids?"

"Fine. They're just fine. Thank the Lord. Lucie Marie?" I heard a voice in the background and the quick muffling sound of a hand placed over the phone. From far away Mabel's voice called to someone, "She ain't got no idear." Then Mabel returned to the phone, "Sugar? Maybe I need to talk to your husband? Is your husband there, sugar?"

"I'm a single woman now, Mabel."

"I'm sorry to hear that, sugar."

"It happens."

"Doncha have no one to help ya?"

"What is it?" Suddenly I remembered it was four in the morning. I remembered Mabel was not a friend, she had been my mother's landlady for over thirty years, and I had not spoken to her for over five years.

"Is something wrong? Has something happened?"

"Are you sittin down, sugar?"

"I'm in bed."

"It's your momma. She just kinda fainted away."

"Is she alive?"

"Oh, my! Now there ain't no cause to be talking that way."

"Is she in the hospital?"

"That's it, sugar. She's in the hospital." Having delivered the bad news, she now relaxed into the easy chatter of a woman who had known me most of my life. "Johnnie called the ambulance, and they took her to the hospital."

"Who's Johnnie?"

"You know, Sam Bevis's boy." Sam Bevis was in his nineties; Johnnie was probably in his seventies. "Your momma's been seeing Johnnie for a good

stretch of time now. Must be . . . they started dat-
ing just after Valentine's Day . . . no, that ain't
right. I do believe your momma was with him 'fore
that. That's right, I recall Johnnie bringin over a
quart of Johnnie Walker on New Year's Eve. He's a
good man. He'd give you the shirt right off his back
and never take no notice. Why, when P. T. and Dale
left for California, he lent them his Ford. Ya know,
the one he was so proud of?"

"I don't think I remember Johnnie Bevis."

"Oh, sure you do, sugar. He used to go with that
Indian girl Delores. Over in El Reno. They had
some good-lookin half-breed kids, all thems grown
up by now. Delores made sure them kids went to
college. Just the other day I went down to the social
security office to get my check and there, just as big
as you please, was one a them kids sitting 'hind this
big old desk."

"I remember Delores."

"Then you gotta member Johnnie."

"He has a taste for Indian women?"

"Now ya sound just like your momma in one a
her black moods. Ain't nothing wrong with a man
likin his meat on the dark side."

Mabel was going on, "He's been in and outta
town all his life. He did spend some time down in

Clinton, ya know, the penitentiary down there. But he got out and got him that Ford and he only been back once or twice."

"Momma. Do they know what happened to her?"

"I ain't no doctor, sugar. But Johnnie called me from the hospital, and he said they're a reckoning on a stroke."

"A stroke!"

"Now, there ain't no need to go a-scaring yourself. My Uncle Bailey had one a them things. Ya member my Uncle Bailey? He sure was fond a ya. Used to say, ya minded him of Jackie Kennedy. He had one a the purdiest funerals I ever seen. His whole family came. Even his daughter out in Californee. Ya run into her out there?"

"It's a big state, Mabel."

"Ain't that the truth. When he passed on, we had the durnest time getting a her. He went so fast, didn't nobody suspect . . . maybe y'all should come on down. Shoot, it couldn't hurt nothing."

The Oklahoma State Indian Hospital was the newest and biggest Indian hospital in the state. It was tucked in the corner of the mammoth health complex, miles and miles of hospitals and clinics and research laboratories quarantined in the northwest corner with the state capitol and government offices. What, I wondered, came first: the government men or the sickness? I couldn't imagine a better Indian joke, placing the contagions together and hoping they would kill each other off.

The Indian hospital covered almost a square mile of prairie at the junction of two interstate highways. At night travelers were pulled toward the white light of a gigantic cross emblazoned across the full six stories of the main building. From the back seat of the cab I saw it appear at the end of the flat and endless highway and knew the sight would have pleased Momma. The cab pulled to a stop under the cross, and I stepped out into the heat of a thousand lights.

*Las Vegas. Arriving at night, momma at the wheel of our old Chevrolet and me on the passenger side, face pressed against the window, as we entered the city from the black surrounding desert. Suddenly, there was the glare of a powerful electric sun. "They say you can't tell night from day," momma said, and I knew why we had come: We came to see the miracle of something from nothing.*

Comprised of large, blocked interconnecting buildings, the hospital was modern and efficiently planned, with narrow mazelike corridors and directories placed every hundred feet. It was a far cry from the Indian hospitals I had gone to as a child, with their sullen white doctors and their angel-of-mercy sisters giving you the privilege of their time and sympathy, driving each patient further into sickness with gratitude. The hospitals had been army barracks, their walls a pale government green, and the only Indians in the place were in the waiting room, some coughing blood, others dazed by the long wait, even the children hung lifeless from a lap or an arm. In the middle of a waiting room, there had been a large chart: HOW TO DRESS WHEN COMING TO SEE THE DOCTOR. I studied the chart, I wanted to dress right, and any piece of information was appreciated. Over a picture of a man and woman in very fancy dress there was a large $X$; over a picture of a man and woman in pajamas there was a large $X$. I looked around, there was not one person in the room in fancy dress or pajamas. But the sign had said nothing about cowboys boots, so I tucked the boots Lizzie had given me under my chair.

But the smell was the same. Not just the smell of disease and antiseptic, it was the funky smell of sweat, urine, excrement, and fear, mostly fear. "The smell of white people," Lizzie had said, "the smell of people who drank too much milk." The smell, I held my breath, of rotting spirits.

A little woman approached me from the end the corridor. I watched her come, down the green hall, her steps soundless and her face silent. The width of her face and her sallow skin told me she was Indian. Cherokee, maybe. She paused next to me and whispered.

"Are they still killing Indians here?"

"Excuse me?"

The woman slipped passed.

"I'm sorry?" I turned and looked for the woman.

But she had already vanished down another sick green corridor. I caught the sound of a chant, monotonous and repetitive, fading into the hallways of the building.

"Crazy Indians!"

At the Intensive Care desk a nurse pointed to a plaque on the opposite wall and said, "Them there are the visiting hours, from one to three and from seven to nine. Visiting hours have been over for almost two hours. You'll have to come back tomorrow."

"But I've just arrived. I haven't seen my mother

since . . . this thing happened. I came all the way from California. I'd just like to let her know I'm here."

"I'm sorry. We have to live by the rules."

"Can you tell me how she is? Gracie Khatib?"

The nurse picked up a handful of manila folders and thumbed through them. "How're ya spelling that last name?"

"K . . . h . . . a . . . t . . . i . . . b.

"I don't find anyone here under that name."

"Evers. Do you have a Gracie Evers?"

"Yep. Room 310, just around the corner. But," she touched my shoulder with the file, "your momma's not going to know if you're here or not. Whyn't you just go on and get some sleep and come back tomorrow?"

"I'd like her to know I'm here."

"I imagine the good Lord has taken care of that."

"Please?"

"Alright. But don't make any noise. You can stay for fifteen or twenty minutes, longer if you sit still."

With the file she motioned for me to follow her down the corridor. All the doors on either side were open. I heard the beep, beep, beep, and crank of machines, but no sounds of the living. I tried to look inside the rooms but could see only the ends of

29

hospital beds and televisions hanging from the ceiling. In a few rooms the pale light of the television flickered. Now and then, I thought I saw a bundle near the foot of the bed, a few bones wrapped in white sheets. At a door near the end of the corridor, the nurse waited for me.

"Now, don't try to disturb her. She can't hear you."

Slowly I approached the woman in the bed. Red lights from the machines over her head pulsated across the dark room. I watched her body disappear into darkness, and then resurrect in a luminous red glow. Here, gone, here, gone. Dizziness and nausea threatened, the room spun. Here, gone, here, gone. I closed my eyes and stepped outside. I took a deep breath and reentered. The woman had my mother's dyed yellow hair and heavy body, my mother's pert nose and swollen arthritic hands, but the face was different. I had never seen the face without animation, without laughter, anger, or dream. I had never seen the lips so limp and thin. From moment to moment, they had shaped words and emotion. Even when she became lost in her own stories, when her face and mind went slack with the past, her eyes burned across the silence.

30

*I wait. She stares into the wall behind me. I wait. Sometimes in the middle of a sentence, in the middle of a story, she drifts into her own dream. I learned to wait, learned to respect the suspension of talk and breath, while she walks through her dream. Then, from somewhere below, she remembers me and continues her story.*

I stood over her bed and waited. I watched her flick in and out of the red light and waited for her to remember me and surface. I took her cold hand in mine and ran my fingers over her arthritic joints. All those years of picking cotton and hard living, she said.

*"I was pickin cotton, when ya was born. Twelve hours a day in that Oklahoma sun. Without nobody a help but your Auney. And she needed help herself. Going from place to place, living on nothing but beans. And singing "Amazing Grace" from sunup to sundown. A whole field of cotton pickers singing "Amazing Grace." Their hands a-bleeding and calloused. Lookit here, ya think people are born with these kind a hands? All crooked and feeling like the bottom a somebody's shoe. I knowed one thing when ya was born, I knowed I didn't wanna pick no more cotton. Liked to a killed me. Both a y'all.*

31

I tried to slip her wedding ring over the swollen joint. "Arthritis," she said, "they'll have a cut this off a me." Once, she had made love and given birth. Once, she had loved to stomp dance, square dance, any kind of dance with drums and a fiddle. And she loved to talk. In my teens, when we lived alone, she would wake me hours before the sun rose. "Rise and shine!" she called from the kitchen, "Rise and Shine!" she called above my pallet. Already, she had had coffee and several cigarettes, already she wanted bright talk and confidences. I sat there, half asleep, while she forced us through the morning's story: her life, Auney's life, her mother's life, Lizzie's life. We never spoke of my life, we knew I had no story. Sometimes, in the middle of recollecting, she would suddenly remember me and say, "Ya mind me a myself." Her claim, my sudden visibility, changed the story for a moment. Only a moment, for we both knew I was biding my time, waiting for my moment of choice.

My mother did not choose and so I had to. All her life she had wanted to run away, slip into some magical and quick life, and so I took the first man leaving town. I flew fast and free, only stopping, when I grew tired or unsure, to whisper "Momma." In hard times, I, too, searched the moon for a mother's face.

My blood carries the worry and wear that made her middle-aged at thirty and old at forty. Any minute the Oklahoma sun could burn my face into hide and wrinkles, any minute the bloat and fatigue could fill my body. Already, the mirror catches her. Only some caution, some reticence, keeps me from exhausting all flesh and heart. But any minute, in the flash of a final disappointment. . . .

Every year I become more Indian, my hair darkens, my eyes grow fierce and still. Slowly, the blood rises, dragging me into its silence. I try to speak, to force words through thick memory, confounding the blood with pirouettes of talk. Every year the blood grows stronger, every year I come a little closer to Lucie who, sitting under the kitchen table, heard her mother tell Auney about Lizzie's death and slipped into months of fearful silence.

I began to pray.

*Y'all look better'n me, she said, y'all have a easier life. That Christmas I sent her a hundred-dollar jar of anti-wrinkle cream. She covered her face with fistfuls of the magic lanolin. She gave her hair a fresh dye and, anxious to have the full effect, she followed with a tight perm the same afternoon. Her hair burned and fell out. She tied a kerchief around her bald head and returned the jar to me.*

*It's too late for me, she said.*
Too late.

Unconscious, Gracie Evers was not an attractive woman. The wrinkles laid heavier in their folds, the eyes sunk in their bags, and without her teeth, the cheeks collapsed into a moist crevice. Sometimes, if there were no men around, Gracie took out her teeth and smoked cigarette after cigarette, her gums locked hard around the filter and her wide smile stretching from gum to gum.

But there was something else, something besides the teeth missing. And then I knew. She was not snoring, that was it. My mother snored like an infantryman, the rasping wide big-mouthed buzz of the very, very tired. She stood twelve hours behind the cafeteria counter and when she came home, she soaked her feet and passed into sleep. Her boyfriends complained they were unable to sleep, most did not spend a second night. Now, only the machinery, breathing and beeping, filled the room with sound. Hypnotically, the bellows next to the bed expanded and collapsed with perfect and silent air, the fluids ticked into her nose and wrist, and the monitors above the bed pulsed the red glow through the room.

I was mesmerized by the machines, her breathing slowed to the bellows, her heart beat to the strobing red light, her body surrendered to the mechanics, the monotony of sustaining and registering life. I watched the bubbles of clear liquid travel through the plastic tubing into Gracie's arm, watched the final suspended drop pause before it fell, carrying sugared water into an inert body. Somehow my loud and vulgar mother had been subdued and sacrificed to this steady drip of fluids.

*Beat the drum slowly . . . don't . . . stop . . . too . . . fast.*

I watched, her body flashing and disappearing, hearing only the suck and gasp of machines. Here, death would not be the performance she had rehearsed again and again. Here, she was outside the story, simply a heavy prop in death's solo act. Here, there would be no stories of pain endured and fear conquered, only the data of life ending as it had ended billions of times before. For my mother, for whom everything was personal, this was not personal. I watched, unable to turn my eyes from the flickering final drop as it teetered just outside the enlarged bruised vein, then the nausea rose, and I fled the room.

"Lizzie wouldn't go to the Indian sanitarium in Talihina. She said, those were places for dying. For white dying, not Indian dying. And she stayed right there. Coughing up hankerchiefs of blood. The TB had her real bad."

Auney hacked on a long smoker's cough.

"But she wouldn't leave. She went to see Alice Six-killer, that medicine woman over in Muskogee. That one she took you to when you had that turrible diarrhea. Alice Sixkiller saved your life many times, girlie, so don't you go acting like we're a bunch a dumb Indians and yer Miss Perfect. Hear?"

"I don't think she meant that, Grace."

"I saw that smirk."

"I was laughing about the diarrhea. How can anyone die of diarrhea?"

"Why don't you ask them doctors at the Indian hospital? You believe them. And they couldn't do no more than wring their hands." My mother wagged her finger at me. "Sister, someday you're gonna be too smart for your own good. Someday, you member my words. Someday, ya gonna understand what I'm talking about."

I unlocked the front door to my mother's house and stepped inside. The house was dark and smelled of tobacco and rotting flesh. The living room was

36

furnished in poor folk renaissance: plastic covered the red velvet couch and chairs, the coffee table was an imitation wagon wheel and cellophane still protected the lamp shades from dust.

*"What's this doing here?" With one pull, my mother-in-law's manicured hand ripped the plastic and dropped it on the floor. She looked at me. "You need to throw that out."*

All of it was from my mother's third and most prosperous marriage to Donny Khatib, a Lebanese hairdresser. They had been an odd couple. They shared the same birthday, or so Donny swore on his naturalization papers, but Gracie looked twenty years older than her husband. He was bone thin and less than five feet tall. Gracie was just over five feet but close to three hundred pounds. But, when he beat her, she collapsed like a child in front of him. He blackened her eyes, broke chairs and coke bottles over her head, and if he was really angry, he unscrewed the leg from the coffee table and came after her with that. I was married then, but I heard about the beatings. In the early morning, while he slept off his meanness, Momma whispered into the phone, "I guess I should count myself lucky.

Ain't nothing broken 'yond repair. And he don't drink and don't run around with women."

Three years after they were married, Donny was walking down Franklin Avenue when two seven-year-old boys, playing next to the curb, looked up and called him a nigger. He reached down and threw one of the boys against the telephone pole. Again and again, he slammed the child's head against the pole. Again and again, until a neighbor woman came running out of her house with a sawed-off shotgun.

"Freeze!" She came right up behind him and stuck the gun into his back. "You sar-r-ry dog! I'll send you straight to hell in less time 'n take ya to pee your pants."

The child recovered, and Donny served seven years at Clinton. Auney moved back in with Momma. Among the three of us, he became known only as "that sar-r-ry dog."

But, for a while, Donny and Momma had found prosperity. Earle, a good old fella from Ferris, let them set up two barber's chairs in the corner of his laundromat. Momma figured people had nothing to do while waiting for their clothes to wash and dry and might want to get their hair cut to pass the time. And they did a good business, earning enough to buy furniture "in cash" and replace the old Chevrolet "on time."

Until he came to the States in his late forties, Donny had been a houseboy to American executives living in Beirut. They taught him to love America and how to pack a suitcase. He shaved, trimmed his employer's hair, and snipped the hairs in ears and nose. Momma had always dyed her black hair a bright yellow blonde and, on the side, she had run a kitchen parlor, dying and perming friends' hair for a small sum. She mixed her own blonde dye, a heavier dose of peroxide and platinum tint, and called it scalping.

Auney was scalped through the entire rainbow of blondes. Her hair burned, frizzed, and faded, but it would not take a color. Momma smothered Auney's hair in petroleum jelly, but it remained thin, limp, dull, the indeterminate color of her sallow skin. "That Indian blood sure is ornery," Momma said with each failure. She had better luck with me. In my junior and senior years in high school, I was a redhead. Well, almost. Where Auney's hair lost all color, mine took a high brassy pitch. She shaved my eyebrows and taught me to circle my eyes with a heavy black pencil, to walk with my chest forward, but I felt conspicuous, a plain girl disguised as a pretty one, and washed the pencil off, closing my arms tightly across my chest.

"What're y'all ashamed of, girl? Look like ya don't wanna be a woman." But I could not keep my arms from my chest or my mouth closed. And I bit my nails to the quick. Momma shook her head and said, "Look like ya don't have no sense atall."

With a final warning, she left me to myself. "You're plain, ya better be smart."

My mother had three husbands, many women and men friends. Once they moved on, though, she lost touch and interest. But she kept every material object that ever crossed her path. Every crevice in the living room was crammed with the souvenirs of living. Her second husband, a slow and unhappy trucker from Abilene, made her a special set of hanging shelves for her knickknacks. She traveled by knickknack. Without ever having left the state, she had a cake dish with Niagara Falls, a bronze cable car from San Francisco, an Elvis pillbox, and a lighter in the shape of the Washington Monument. Next to the shelf she had hung a framed high school diploma from Clinton Penitentiary in the name of Johnnie Bevis.

"At least he graduated. Momma was always a sucker for education."

I turned on more lights and stood between the kitchen and the living room. The old kitchen table had been replaced by an oval white formica dinette with four plastic chairs. The cellophane was still wrapped around their floral seats. The end tables straddling the couch matched the dark imitation wood of the wagon wheel coffee table. A pair of ceramic dalmations stood guard on either side of the television; on top, two bright parakeets perched. Smoky blue-glassed ashtrays tied sofa and tables and television together.

"I got me some real furniture," I hear Momma tell me. "I'm a sick to death a people's throwaways."

*Trash days we cruise the better neighborhoods. Momma's at the wheel, Auney's glued to the window. Two carrions in the front seat. I slump in the back, their quickest thief.*

*"These people got so much," Momma says, turning into a quiet tree-lined street. "They don't even know what they're a-throwing away."*

*"Naw, they sure don't."*

*"Lookit there." She spots a promising pile of boxes. The Packard glides to the the curb, and Auney and I dart from*

*the car, shift quickly through the rubbish, and load a box of cracked china into the back seat. Auney grabs a fistful of wire hangers. "Wait!" I call and return with my arms full of books.*

*"Ifn ya had as good an eye for useful things as ya do for them books, our trash-hunting days'd be over."*

*"I reckon she finds something in 'em," I hear Auney say.*

*"What's she's finding ain't gonna do her no worldly good."*

*"Ain't no telling what a body's gonna need."*

"Ain't no telling," I hear myself say as I walked into the back of the house.

The bedroom furniture was a blond wood, a hulky dresser and bed with a heavy headboard filled the room from wall to wall. The smell of talcum and musk hung in the room. In the small bedroom, the one Gracie called her sewing room, there was a heap of dirty or clean unsorted clothes. I picked up a few things, looked around to see a place to put them. Helplessly, I started this way and that and then threw them back on the floor.

I closed the door tight and walked into the kitchen. The refrigerator contained half a pack of brown 'n' serve breakfast sausages, eggs, and four hamburger buns.

*Momma hated uppity Indians. Uncle Henry was an unpretentious hardworking farmer, married to an Indian woman, Bertha. "They think they're better'n everbody else. I seen inside their icebox and they didn't have but butter and bread. Feeding all them kids on bread and butter." I knew that's all we had in our icebox but I checked anyway. Inside was half a stick of margarine and some slices of white bread. Uncle Henry's family didn't sound so poor to me.*

I opened the cabinets, Momma had gotten worse. There were hundreds of cans of vienna sausages, spam, tuna, macaroni and cheese, and so forth. Suddenly, after years of living on nothing, she had become afraid of starving. Or maybe she had realized, after all these years, just how hungry she was.

*The last week of every month, I walked across town to Roy's General Store. He is the only storekeeper to give credit, and Momma sends me to ask. I walk in the gullies, down side streets, under huge billboards, with my list. Grits, bacon, beans, bread, and cigarettes.*

*"Git a little something for yourself," Momma says.*

*I walk quickly. On the way back I will linger, dipping my fingers into the jar of peanut butter and rubbing the gluey texture against the top of my mouth until it becomes sweet cream.*

43

*I hand my list to Mr. Roy. He reads it, smiles, and I wait while he collects our food. He comes back with a jar of peanut butter.*

*"Ya sure ya wouldn't like a ice cream sandwich?"*

*"No, sir. No, thank ya, Mister Roy."*

*He adds our purchases, slides the bill across the counter, and I write my careful ten-year-old signature on the credit slip. I take up the brown bag and turn to leave.*

*"Thank ya, Mister Roy."*

*"Ain't ya forgetting something?"*

*I freeze.*

*"Ain't no way to be treating your uncle Roy. Come on back here and give your uncle Roy a kiss. Come on, he ain't a-gonna eat ya."*

Hundreds of cans, stacked one on the other, haphazard in size and content. This house has known a lot of hunger.

*"Ain't ya forgetting something?"*

Sometimes, when Melvin touched me, I remembered. When he fell asleep, I went down to the kitchen and ate. Potato chips, ice cream, kosher salami sandwiches, I took pleasure in my choices and the sleep that followed.

I study my mother's booty and consider my

choices. I reach for a can of macaroni and cheese and change my mind. The sweet taste of Vienna sausages, the memory of their thick slick jelly. A can of hominy? We ate it cold, from the can with a spoon. Tuna fish? With mayonnaise, chopped onions, and pickles on white bread, a special luxury. Now she had cans and cans of rotting fish. Sardines, smoked oysters, even kippers. Rich people's foods.

When she retired from the cafeteria, she went back to babysitting and cleaning houses. She loved her employers—"Rich people just like you an' me"— their children, and their stories. She told their stories as if they belonged to her: she told how Mrs. Weiss escaped the Nazis, through Russia and China and over the Pacific to San Francisco; she told how Mrs. Peterson had been married before, to a no-good stuck-up man, and how her children didn't have anything to do with her; and she lamented little Michael's medical condition, "Poor thing, can't take no solid foods, ever thing'd gotta be put in the blender first." When they forgot to leave her thirty dollars on the hall table, Momma worried over their hard times.

We drove past their houses, Momma slowing down and pointing, giving me a tour through each room, proud of the time it took to clean it. I never

45

met Mrs. Weiss or Mrs. Peterson, although I did meet poor little Michael, but I knew their lives and carried their stories. In many ways, they were more real to me than my grandmother or Lizzie.

I learned my mother's respect for education and white ambition from those drives past the Weiss and Peterson homes. But when I returned, a competent Weiss or Peterson, Momma and Auney only shook their heads and giggled.

"Ain't she something?"

"It do beat all."

"What?" I demanded. With my first charge card, I had purchased a beige linen suit. Straight skirt, double-breasted, a turtleneck dickey.

"Don't git your back up," Momma said. "Your Auney and me's just having us a little fun."

They collapsed on the table in laughter.

"I'm making something of myself."

Again, they went down in laughter.

"Ya'd best go on back to that store. They done sold ya a shirt and kept the sleeves."

"What ya call that thing?" Auney asked, wiping her eyes. "I done seen ever thing."

Hillbillies, I heard my mother say. I began to arrange my mother's cans, size on size, guessing at the age, sometimes the contents. I took down the first shelf, considered the mess and grew tired. Even when I became a teacher, Momma acted as if I had lied about college, my degree, my work. She asked no questions, walked around my achievements with a careful disbelief.

*"Will you come to my class?"*
*"Will* they *let me come?"*
*"I teach the class."*
*"Maybe you need to ask somebody."*

And she didn't come. She waited in my office at the university, the door closed, sitting in the furthest corner of the room. No doubt ready to produce proof, on the spot, that she was no burglar.

I looked around the kitchen and glanced into the living room. Something was there. Something had moved, rearranging the air and space around it. I walked into the bedrooms and returned to the kitchen. I was not alone. Some heaviness hung and waited, around the corner, behind a door. I felt it waiting to surprise. I opened the kitchen window. Shoo, I said. Go on, go on. I went into the living room and opened the windows. I felt it circling through the house, slamming against the windows, as it fought to stay close.

47

I feel her fear, chasing her into a frenzied hiding and hunkering. Waiting, the sadness holding its breath, she doesn't want to leave the house.

*"I was at the sink a-washing the dishes,"* the hair on my arms stands up when Momma begins this story, *"all of a sudden, a hand reaches for the dishrag. I'm a-thinking it's yours, Missy, and I swat it. But the same time's I'm a-swatting it, I sees it's a old hand, a wrinkled-up old hand, as sure as I'm a-sitting here a-talking to ya. The very next day word reaches me, Lizzie done died a week ago."*

I returned the cans to the first shelf, reading labels, concentrating on the details of spelling and grammar. If I lifted my eyes or turned too quickly, I knew I would see her and would not be able to unsee her. She watched and waited for her chance. The hairs stand up on my arms, and I turn my back to the table. My eyes down, on the labels, I try to whistle.

> *A whistling girl and a crowing hen*
> *will come to no good end.*

Go on . . . shoo! I keep my eyes down and wish her away.

I had wished her away many times before. Once, to a schoolmate, who told her mother, who told

48

Gracie, I said I had been adopted. The short fat woman, working in the cafeteria, was not my real mother, my real mother lived in New York, the daughter of an industrialist, forced to give up her only child because of a teenage pregnancy. Momma was hurt but not angry. She blamed all those books.

On Sundays Momma and Auney went to the Southern Baptist church, and I walked two miles to the Catholic church on the other side of town. I had fallen in love with the rituals and rich purple garments. At age ten, I was baptized Antoinette. When Momma heard about my lie, she and Auney drove me to confession and waited, the entire church dead silent while I hiccuped my way through the act of contrition. *Forgive—hiccup—me Father—hiccup—for I have—hiccup—sinned.* And I hiccuped straight through the penance. Nothing helped, not water, not holding my breath, not even the drawl of Momma and Auney's steady gossip from the back of the church.

She came to my wedding. She stepped out of the cab dressed for the event, a tea-length multilayered turquoise chiffon, her hair freshly peroxided and tightly permed. Her shoes and purse had, obviously, not taken the first dye and were now in the "anyone's guess" color scheme. And the hat, Lord have mercy, was a wide-brim straw with a sequined turquoise horse in the front. I watched from the picture window as three hundred pounds of turquoise, with gloves, tried to find the front door of my in-laws' North Shore home. Melvin's grandmother, coming in from the back, caught a look at Gracie, shrieked, and had to be rushed into the back room by Melvin's parents. They seated Gracie on the bride's side, along with the black maid, and she sobbed through the entire ceremony. When the guests in cool summer linen stood up to cry *mazel tov*, Momma let go a heart-stopping cry, "My baby!" The black maid patted her on the shoulder.

Passing by the buffet table, I heard a matron in pearls say, "I never met a real Indian before."

Momma was loading her plate with shrimp du jong.

"My momma was a full-blooded Cherokee. She had hair down to her waist. This far." She placed the spoon just above her wide ass. "Indians don't git many shrimps. There ain't nothing I loves better'n shrimps."

"Oy vey," I groaned and reached back into Momma's horde for a can of tuna. I beat eggs and slid the frying pan onto the largest burner. I coated it with a spoon of bacon fat from the Crisco can on the stove. Tuna egg omelette. Momma's only recipe: take any available items, beat, and fry.

*Marry a rich man and you'll pay for every cent.*

Go on . . . shoo!

I slide an ashtray and her cigarettes and lighter to the end of the table and begin to eat.

It wasn't my fault I hated her then. A child would have had more sense. And the wedding was not the end of it. The next morning Gracie had called to meet me for breakfast. Melvin's father told her to check out of the hotel and take a cab to the airport. No one told me she had called. Indeed, my new family was too polite to mention my mother; even the wedding album graciously ignored her. And I was grateful, as grateful as an orphan, for their good manners. It took me many bad years to realize I was an unmentionable too.

There was a knock on the door. Through the kitchen window I saw Mabel peering into the other side of the glass. When I opened the door, Mabel walked in in her robe and nightgown and began clucking her tongue.

"I guess ya seen your momma ain't changed her housekeeping habits."

"She never was fond of it."

"Fond? Why, sugar, yer momma'd put a rat to shame." She saw the look on my face and laughed. "Shoot, ain't your momma's fault. All them Evers was like that, they couldn't pour piss out of a boot with the directions written on the bottom."

"Mabel, I know you don't mean no harm, but . . . ," I searched for an objection.

"There you are, smart as whip." Mabel pointed to the photograph over the couch. I stood, a proud five years old in my beloved leopard skin coat and cowboy boots, next to Lizzie. Behind us was Momma's pride, the new black Packard. Mabel looked from the picture to me. "You do look like your momma. Someday, y'all look like sisters."

"That's the picture from the cutest baby contest."

"I know, sugar, your momma told me all 'bout it. Your momma went and saw it right down here at the Chickasaw. You remember the Chickasaw?" She peered close to the picture and then back at me again. "You do favor her. You got 'em dark eyes and . . . ya got her look. She never did look happy. Always looked like she was seeing something disagreeable. I keep a-telling her, 'Your face is a-gonna freeze that way if ya keep it up.'"

"I think I need to go to bed."

52

"Ya know, your momma never a figured why that old Injun woman bought you them fancy clothes — just look at that there coat — and took you to Lawton for the contest. I hear when the TB took her she just kept to herself. Wild horses couldna dragged her to town from that farm." I smiled. I knew things about Mabel. I knew how she had gotten the money to buy these two houses, I knew enough to be the storyteller of her life. "Your momma said that old Injun woman didn't like white people. She hurt your momma's feelings turrible. It ain't natural, her turning her back on yer momma thataway. I hear a lot of Injuns can't trust their own families. My own girl. You remember Lula Faye? She run off with this carousel operator. Now she's got . . ."

"Lizzie never did . . . I really am tired, Mabel," I said and opened the door.

"Listen, sugar, you had yourself a bad day. All that flying and running to the hospital. I'm amazed you're still walking around."

"I think I need to go to bed."

"Sure, honey, you do that. God helps thems that helps themselves." She turned on the porch. "How's your momma? She gonna be alright?"

*Machines pump and bubble and tease, bellows hold-*

*ing, suctioning, and returning breath.* Are they still killing people here?

"Did Momma want to go to the Indian hospital?"

"Sugar, she was unconscious. There weren't no asking done."

"Yeah, right." I wondered if Mabel thought I was one of them dumb Evers. "I don't know how she is. I don't know what to do."

"Trust the Lord, sugar. And get some sleep."

I watched Mabel cross the yard to her house. She had crossed that yard thousands of times, giving a yell and showing up at our kitchen table for coffee and gossip. Once a year she brought her cinnamon rolls. Mostly, she ate our food and drank our coffee. No one made phone calls then, and it would have been unneighborly to suggest someone call before showing up. During the last bare week of the month, Momma would complain, "She been eating me outta house and home. An' she wants rent too." She cursed her stinginess and swore "that old whore" would never step a foot inside our house "till Hell done freezes over." But when Mabel showed up, momma forgot her anger and hollered to me, "Git your aunt Mabel some coffee."

Mabel disappeared into her house. "I remember

Lula Faye," I said into the quiet night. "She was the town whore, slept with every Injun and nigger in town." I felt the heaviness in the house lift with laughter. The Lula Faye I remembered was an ugly pale thing, skin and bones, with a craving for bananas. "They put the meat on you," she told me. I couldn't eat a banana for years.

I never felt so alone. Many years ago I gave up Oklahoma without so much as a glance, not returning even when Auney died last year. I learned to draw my words together, to speak rapidly and convincingly, to learn the good manners of middle-class ambition. Here, in a world that would never concede to change, I felt a loneliness never known in New York or Boston or San Francisco.

*There ain't nothing for ya here, Auney said.*
*Why?*
*Her face went slack and her eyes said, Look at me. Look at me. Is this what you want? She blew a perfect circle of smoke and laughed.*

I took the covers off Momma's bed and made a pallet on the living room floor. As a child my bed consisted of a pallet, a pillow and blankets rolled up in the corner of the room. On some nights I take the covers off my bed in Boston or New York and sleep on the floor. God entered my life with Lizzie. After Lizzie I knelt and prayed every night, I knelt and prayed every morning. For over thirty years I've been kneeling and praying, kneeling and praying, "Please God, don't let anything happen."

Sometimes, I sat on the porch and searched the moon for Lizzie's face. "I'll be a-watching ya from the moon," Grandma had told Momma and Auney. I never saw Lizzie's face in the moon, perhaps it held only my grandmother's face, but once I heard her call my name, "Lu-u-cie," from the back of the house. I ran to the spot as fast as I could, but there was no one there.

The women in my family raised me with a proud faith in the Cherokee and God. Now I was a little ashamed of both. They were formulas of being, avenues in a claim to spirituality. Everyone believed in God and everyone, it seemed, had a little Cherokee blood. Both were ways of living without meaning, without history. I have always been confused by those who talk and talk of their religious beliefs or Indian identity. As far back as I can remember, I belonged to a secret society of Indian women, meeting around a kitchen table in a conspiracy to bring the past into the present. I listened, their stories settling forever in my blood, and I knew the stories were told and told not for carrying but for keeping.

They heard, and they taught me to hear, the truth in things not said. They listened, and they taught me to listen, in the space between words. *"Ifn a man gotta tell ya what he's got,"* my momma said, *"he done already lost it."*

*"This here's the Reverend Tom Cottonmouth. Speakin' to ya from the national I Wannabe a Cherokee network in Tulsa, Oklahoma. The Cherokees loves y'all and needs your help. If youse got Cherokee blood a-running through your veins, no matter how distant, no matter how pre-e-e-posterous, no matter how recent, the Cherokees loves y'all.*

*Ifn your having a little tribal uncertainty, ifn the drum is telling ya the Apache, the Choctaw, the Osage is not fer you, ifn ya say Iroquois and the white man thinks you're from the Middle East, then come on down to the Cherokee Meeting House.*

*Ifn y'all had bad credit, a turn a bad luck, think to yourselves, Indian brothers and sisters, maybe y'all need a new identity. An' ya can have it right here, no questions asked an' no references needed. Y'all had grandmommas, ain't no more needed than that.*

*For just a ten-dollar bill, no checks please, we'll send ya a authentic certificate of Cherokee blood. And wait,*

*Indian brothers and sisters, ifn ya do that 'fore midnight tonight, we'll also send ya a genuine rock from the Cherokee Nation. That's right, a genuine rock from our sacred Cherokee land.*

*Send us your money now, Indian brothers and sisters. Do it now, brothers and sisters. Don't be left outta the new Cherokee Nation.*

*Cherokee. We mean Indian.*

Around the kitchen table, Momma and Auney talked of Indian women and their lives as children and young women. But the talk stayed between them. I listened. My understanding was measured by silent attention and respect. They spoke of my relatives too, but I did not own the story yet, and it would have been shameful and disrespectful to claim it. "Remember" resonated in every word, but remembering meant remembering through the storyteller.

I have tried to remember my life outside the remembering of that kitchen table. I have tried to circumvent the storyteller and know my life with an easy Indian memory, but I knew no Indian princesses, no buckskin, no feathers, no tomahawks. The Indians in westerns confused and frightened me. My mother and aunt chose high heels over mocassins; they would have chosen blue eyes over black eyes. I have tried to know Momma, Auney, and Lizzie as Indian women, but all that surfaces is tired, worn-out women, stooped from picking cotton and the hard work of tenant farming. I know women burnt by the hot Oklahoma sun and wasted by their men, women scared into secrets, women of a solid and steady patience. But, mostly, I know them by their hunger to talk.

I listened.

"What's it like being Indian?" friends ask. I want to respond, "What's it like being alive?" But they demand difference, want to believe in Indian transcendence and spirituality, as if their own survival depended on the Indian. I wish I had Indian stories, crazy and wild romantic vignettes of a life lived apart from them. Anything to make myself equal to their romance. Instead I can offer only a picture of Momma's rented house, a tiny flat two-bedroom shack in a run-down part of town.

"It means living like this," I would say, knowing I've told them nothing, sure I've kept my secrets.

*Whispers and movement wake me in the middle of the night. A large fat pink man stands just inside the opened door. My mother is in front of him. In the moonlight I see her large nude ass and the roll of fat hanging on her hips.*

*She is whispering, something urgent and desperate. I hear her ask, "The car payment's okay this month?" The pigman grunts. A breeze comes through the door and blows the smell of their sweat and whiskey into my corner. He leaves. Momma comes and lies next to me on my pallet. I pretend to be asleep.*

I removed the picture of Lizzie and me from the wall and took it to my pallet. I studied Lizzie's face. She was a dark severe woman and looked more like a Quaker than an Indian. There's no foolishness in her face, no laugh lines or an easy smile, but hers is not a mean face. Lizzie's story, it occurs to me, is somewhere in that leopard coat. She never mentioned, before or after the event, the beautiful baby contest to Lucie. But a week after the advertisement went up in the window of the town store, they were on a bus to Oklahoma City to find Lucie a dress to wear when "them movie men" came to Davis. She packed fried chicken and biscuits for lunch and dinner, pinned the egg money inside her bra, and laid out their best Sunday clothes.

"Would ya look at that?" Lizzie said as the bus traveled through the Arbuckle mountains and into the flat plains of the state. "Good Lord almighty, I'd almost forgot what it looked like."

They went across the street from the bus terminal to Woolworth's. The store was as large and noisy as a train station. Lizzie hung back, shamed and disoriented by the size and racket of the place, and Lucie took charge, walking up and down the aisles with proud experience. The leopard coat was the first thing she really saw, a glossy spotted pattern with black cuffs and collar and three big gold buttons. She put it on over her pink dress and smiled up at Lizzie.

"It sure do look pretty. But I ain't sure they's a-gonna want little girls in coats."

"Did they say no coats?"

"I guess they didn't say nothing about that."

Lucie turned, took a few steps down the aisle, and turned on point. "I feel like Shirley Temple."

Now, studying the picture, I can see that the coat had not fit well. Even her small four-year-old body was too large for the thing. The wonderful black cuffs ended well before the wrists, and the hem of the pink dress hung inches below the coat. But there they stood, in front of Momma's Packard, two girls proud of their purchase. On his first and final visit to Momma's house, Melvin examined the picture and declared, "You were a ragamuffin!" With that one word, the leopard coat left me. Flying into the past, a shameful thing, an unworthy thing, it caught on its false promise and I never wore it with pride again.

Lucie looks straight into the camera, a pleased rebel in braids, leopard, and cowboy boots. I try to imagine myself into her, try to take her magic and stories into my tired life, but I cannot get beyond the image.

*"Jump, jump, jump," I whisper.*

But she stands at the edge, facing me.

*"You talk in your sleep," Melvin said, the second morning of our honeymoon.*

*"I do not."*

*"Yes, you do. You talk in your sleep."*

*"No."*

*"Yes."*

*"What . . . did . . . I . . . say?"*

*"You said, 'I don't wanna travel back with them, all's I wanna do is be with you.'"*

*"'I don't wanna travel back with them, all's I wanna do is be with you?'"*

*"Yeah. Isn't that funny?"*

*Traveling back . . .*

WHEN LUCIE WAS FOUR YEARS OLD, J. D. moved into their tiny house. He was a tall, red-faced, ugly man with a short temper, a supply sergeant with a good salary, stationed at Fort Sill. He was, as Momma and Auney said, a "drinking man." He took his first shot of whiskey in his morning coffee, drank beer behind the PX during the day, and then started his "serious" drinking when he got home.

In the beginning Momma could not believe her luck. J. D. supervised the commissary and PX deliveries and helped himself, and everyone on duty, to whatever passed him on the commissary loading dock. He backed his Ford up to the dock, packed his trunk, and covered the boxes with an old army blanket. Several times a week he came home with cases of beer and bottles of Jack Daniels and cartons of Kools and Winstons. On odd days he'd turn up with boxes of cookies or cereal or canned soups or sides of beef. They turned the sewing room into something of a warehouse, put up shelves, and rented a long commercial freezer. Momma invited Mabel "to help herself" until she found out Mabel was selling the beer and cigarettes at half cost.

"Lordy, Lordy," Auney said. She walked around the tiny stuffed room in disbelief. Momma packed Tom's car with boxes of cigarettes and beer, two dozen porterhouses, and ten five-pound cans of coffee. Auney backed out into the street, waving and laughing like a child who's found Santa Claus.

J. D. brought home a two-gallon jar of peanut butter, government issue. He sat it before the child and joked, "What're ya gonna give me for this?" Lucie looked up at him, saw him sway a little in his uniform, then dropped her eyes.

"Ain't ya gonna say nothing?"

"I don't know," the child finally said.

"You don't know? Ya hear that Gracie? Ya hear how this half-breed a yours talks to me? I ain't a-gonna take her sass. Ya hear?"

Lucie cringed. Her mother was drinking too. "I take it all a time. I can't do nothing with her."

"I don't aim to let no bastard baby show me no disrespect. Ya hear?"

"Maybe ya can learn her to mind. I done tried all I knowed."

In the best of moods, he teased the child, mimicking her short quick movements as she went about her chores, tugging at the end of a plate as she tried to clear the table.

"Stop!" she cried. "Stop!" he cried.

She pushed a chair up to the sink to do the dishes, and he knelt at the sink, flapping his hands about the water.

"Don't!" she cried. "Don't!" he cried.

In the morning her mother yelled and Lucie scampered into the kitchen and made J. D. his coffee and breakfast. She pushed the chair to the sink, filled the percolator, pushed the chair to the stove, measured in the coffee, and lit the back burner. She lit the burner under the skillet, spooned in bacon grease, and fried two eggs. Then she stood against the kitchen cabinet, her head barely reaching the counter, with her arms crossed on her chest, and watched J. D. stuff a runny egg into his mouth.

"Whatya looking at, big eyes?"

Lucie looked down and said nothing.

"Hey, I'm a-talking to ya! Hey, papoose, I'm a-talking to ya!"

Lucie pushed herself further into the corner.

"What's wrong with you damn Injuns? Don't none of y'all talk?" He slapped his hands together. Lucie flinched from the noise. "Ya look at me when I'm a-talking. Show me respect, here. I'm a-paying the bills and putting food in your mouth. Ya fucking Injun brat."

Lucie wanted to say she wasn't an Injun, not like Lizzie and the rest of those Evers, but if he hit her and she cried, Gracie would come roaring out of the bedroom and hit her again for waking her up. She bit her lip. Every morning this struggle went on between them, and finally Lucie would look up and J. D. would say, "Can't ya smile?"

One morning Lucie fried the yolks of his eggs too hard. He sat there bouncing his fork off the rubbery yolks, then dumped them into the garbage bag.

"Make 'em right this time."

J. D. watched and fumed as she fried another pair. She was so nervous she almost fell off the chair, and afterward she squeezed into the corner and watched him eat.

He poured whiskey into his coffee and turned. "Whatya looking at, kid? This ain't no sideshow."

Lucie pulled her hands behind her.

"I asked ya a question. What's wrong, some Injun got your tongue?" J. D. leaned back, hit the table, and roared. "That must be it, Injun's got your tongue."

Lucie put her head down.

"I've a mind to come over there and knock some

sense into your head. T'ain't nothing but Injun trash. Your momma's trash, and you're trash too."

Lucie looked at him, stared at his pitted face.

"Scum," she said.

Her hands flew to her mouth. The sounds of apology were beginning when the fist struck her face. She covered her face as he dragged her across the linoleum by her hair.

"I'm gonna teach ya a lesson you ain't gonna forget. Now'n you shut up or I'm a-gonna make it hard on ya." She tried to swallow her sobs, but they refused to stay down. She saw Momma, sleeping. He tightened his hand around her face and locked her mouth. With his other hand he unbuttoned her nightgown and fished it down her shoulders. Her body lay lifeless beneath him as he pulled her cotton panties down.

*There was the flash of pain and the taste of vomit. In the same dizzying flash the pain took the fear. I know now that fear left me that morning. I began to plan to kill him. I kept my eyes down, I didn't look at him, but I watched for my chance.*

*I sat up on my pallet, looked around in the darkness, and waited. My breathing slowed, listening for the*

*sound again. The creak of a step, the brush of trousers*
*against the wall, the opening of a bedroom window. I*
*heard the kitchen curtain flap and got up and closed the*
*window.*

*I wrapped the pallet around me and huddled in the*
*corner. The street light shone in the living room and*
*kitchen windows. The house looked better with just a*
*trace of light, anyone could have lived there. There was a*
*sheen to the place, luminescence from the plastic covers.*
*Even the cellophane on the lights and kitchen chairs*
*shone. I sat straight, very still, waiting in the darkness.*
*Outside I heard steps on the road, then a drunken voice*
*zigzagging through a song.*

> *How high's the water, Momma?*
> *Six feet high and rising.*
> *How high's the water, Papa?*
> *Seven feet high and rising.*

Her mother was in the bathroom. Lucie could
hear her throwing up, hear her voice as it called
from the floor, "How high's the water, Momma?"
and the sound of her retching, again, into the toilet.
Lucie knew the door was locked, only the voice
careered through the house, sick with despair, carrying a warble of resistance in its persistent question, "How high's the water, Momma?"

69

J. D. had walked out. "I don't aim to stay in no house with that brat, always looking at me like she got no respect. You hear me? You get rid of that brat or I'm a-leaving!"

The next morning Gracie made breakfast and Lucie packed, trying not to look at her mother, for it was her eyes that had gotten her into trouble. She waited on the couch, surrounded by grocery bags stuffed with her few things; at the bottom of one she had pirated a small jar of peanut butter. She had heard a lot of unpleasant things about Lizzie, certainly not a person you could trust to have a jar of peanut butter on hand.

She knew about trips. The summer Momma picked cotton she lived with Auney in her trailer until Uncle Tom said she made too much noise. Auney had made her milk shakes and took her to bingo. Lizzie, she guessed, wouldn't hold with milk shakes or bingo. She was uppity, Momma said.

They drove south to Davis, raising the dust on innumerable back roads. "The backwoods," Gracie sneered. "Take a look around, sister. There are more ignorant people out here than you can shake a finger at."

Lucie looked out the window and saw no people. The land stretched across the plain until it touched the sky. Nothing stood between the land and its meeting. Now and then, the land opened up and Lucie saw the red earth below.

"Does the dirt bleed?" she asked.

"What kinda question is that? Ya know dirt don't bleed. Only people bleed."

"Maybe there's people buried under that dirt?"

"Maybe, sister. Lord knows enough people have died in this state."

The wind beat against the windows, rattling the glass fiercely. "Aha! The witches are trying to get in. I'll have to drive faster. Some a them witches can run faster'n a car."

Lucie slid closer to her mother.

"You seen a witch, Momma?"

"Sure. I seen a witch. Seen witches all the time when I was your age. They love the backwoods. Uncle Jerry knows 'em witches." Gracie laughed. "Since he lost his mind he ain't got the sense to tell a witch from a mule."

Lucie touched her forehead and said, "How's a person lose his mind? Does he get shot?"

"That's one way a doing it. With Uncle Jerry he just . . . well, hell, ya heard the story. I guess ya could just plain say he were just born a Evers."

"Are the Evers witches?"

71

"No, Missy, they's just Indians."

"Was Granma a witch?"

"There's some, I reckon, would call her a witch. She saw things and heard things other people don't. Yer aunt Rozella's like that. But that didn't make my momma no witch. Once, I member, she chased a witch away from our door. This here witch had come up to git us, and Momma took a broom to her. Shoo! shoo! and the witch went flying into the trees."

"Maybe the witch'll git me."

"What's a witch a-gonna do with a troublemaker like you? Naw, ya just too much trouble. 'Sides, I reckon Lizzie'll shoo her away. Gimme that beer on the floor." Lucie picked up the beer, placed it between her legs, and pressed down hard with the opener. "What ya doing, I didn't ask ya . . ." The beer exploded, sending foam up to the ceiling and onto the windows. "Look what ya done. You're always into everthing. Didn't nobody ask ya to . . . don't ya cry or I'll smack ya. Ya hear? Now git something and clean up this mess."

Lucie leaned over the seat and took a dress out of a grocery bag.

"Not that. Ain't ya got no more sense 'n that?" Gracie stretched an arm into the back and came back with a pair of cotton panties. "Here, use this here.

"I told ya not to cry." Gracie sat the beer can on the seat next to her. "It's your own fault, girlie, ya got your nose in everthing. J. D. ain't such a bad man, ya just gotta give a little, that's all. I ask ya to be nice to him. But ya got your own ideas. Always have. You're selfish, always a-doing what ya want outta no thought for me. I don't know where you picked all this stuff up, little Miss Perfect, you barely four years old and trying to tell adults how to behave. Well, you 'bout to meet your match, sister. I shoulda handed ya over to Lizzie years ago, she'd a taken all this holier'n shit right outta ya. I gotta soft spot for you, but ya gotta learn to mind. Your days a milk an' honey are over . . ."

*Now when I recall this scene, I see it from the top of the Packard, moving pictures of my mother's slurred angry face, a beer can propped against the wheel, and Lucie pressed to the window, her legs dangling over the front seat. She knows her mother's anger is not for her but a confidence. She knows her mother's life will feed the red earth, continuing to confuse and take the lives she dreams, and there is nothing she can do but rage against the sacrifice. Already I know I was born here, but it will not*

73

*give birth to me. I listen to my mother and plan where and how I will be born.*

Gracie made a U-turn and followed the road back to a dirt side road. "Lord, this place minds me a Jeeter's place," and she took her foot off the accelerator. "We had a creek, too, right there." She pointed to a space behind the trees. "We was always running off to that creek. It was the only place we could get away from old man Jeeter." She stopped the car. "You hear it? Your Auney thought creeks could talk. We'd come down here an' sit, not one of us saying a word."

The car bumped down the road. On each side, river scrub trees shaded the lane from the hot sun. Now and then there was a gap in the trees, and the car came out into the blinding daylight. Lucie tried to see to the end of the road, but she couldn't see beyond the shade and sun. Suddenly they came out of the trees and pulled up in front of a neat white-shingled farmhouse with a white fence around the front yard.

"Lizzie sure has done wonders with this place. I know she ain't had no help from Uncle Jerry. He's the laziest man God put on this here earth. Jeeter's place didn't look half as nice when your Auney and me was growing up. He wouldn't give no one a nickel unless they earned it five times over."

A small dark woman opened the screen door and stepped to the end of the broad porch, her hand sheltering her eyes from the glare of the high sun as she tried to see inside the Packard. Her eyes landed on Lucie, and the child pulled away from the window.

"You wait here, hear?" Gracie wiped her mouth with her hand, then peered anxiously into the rearview mirror, taking out her compact and mopping the oil from her face. She took out a tube of Red Red and traced the lines of her mouth. "How I look?"

"Okay, I guess."

"Thank ya."

Lucie crawled into the dark recess of the back seat and watched as her mother approached the old woman on the porch. Gracie made gestures of greeting and sang out exclamations of joy, but the old woman watched motionless and silent from the porch, refusing to approach or acknowledge Gracie. An old man in overalls appeared and hung next to the door.

On the porch Gracie hugged the stiff woman. The old man reached out and patted her shoulder.

75

Lucie thought he looked like a wrinkled old child. The old woman pulled her lips tight as her mother's mouth moved fast in explanation, her hands wild in communication. The old man reached out and patted her shoulder. Now and then, she pointed to the car, and Lucie slumped down into the seat.

After an interminable ten or fifteen minutes, the old woman waved Gracie to the side and walked down the steps, down the walk to the gate, right up to the passenger side of the Packard. She rapped against the window and motioned to the child to come out. Lucie climbed into the front seat, looked at the old woman, and shook her head. The woman rapped again, and Lucie opened the door and carefully stepped down into the gravel.

She squirmed under the old woman's eyes, pulling her dress down in back and dusting the dirt from her shoes. She had put on her best pink chiffon dress, the one with many curling layers, a pink bow was tied around her head, and her Buster Browns were laced up. Looking in Gracie's mirror this morning, she had been pleased with her appearance, but under the old woman's eyes, she knew the dress was cheap and common. She studied the hem of the woman's apron, shifting onto one foot, then another. The child looked up at the woman and tried to smile: the old woman was smaller than her mother, but it seemed miles and miles up to the black eyes and wide taut face. Lucie dug one shoe into the gravel.

"Sister, this here's your aunt Lizzie." Gracie stood beside the woman and draped an arm around her shoulders. Her mother looked like a big sloppy dog. "Go on, don't be bashful, give your aunt Lizzie a hug." Lucie dragged the side of her shoe into an *L*. "Now, go on." Gracie pushed her forward. "Don't shame me, go an' give your aunt Lizzie a hug."

"How long ya planning to leave her?" The question had little courtesy in it. It was a request for simple information.

"Just till I can git things straighten out with J. D. He ain't a bad man, he takes real good care of me. I brought ya some things from the commissary over at Fort Sill. He's the supply sergeant. I ain't had to worry none 'bout eating, I can tell ya."

The old woman spit.

"He got any chewing tobackey?"

"Naw, Uncle Jerry, folks don't chew that stuff no more." Gracie opened her purse and took out a pack of cigarettes. "Whyn't ya try a smoke?"

"No, thank ya. I been chewing so long, I'd most miss the taste."

"We ain't so bad off we gotta steal to eat," the old woman said.

"Lizzie . . . Grace's just being neighborly," the old man said and gently waved the cigarette away.

"I ain't a-gonna have stolen goods in my house. I weren't raised thataway, and Grace Evers, your momma didn't raise ya thataway."

"J. D. ain't a bad man," Gracie tried to explain. "Lots a people in the army takes a few things. Why, he's tried real hard to better hisself. And he's tried real hard to be a daddy to sister."

"Is he her daddy?"

"Naw. I only been with him since the summer. His own kids is all grown, and he's tried to be a daddy to sister. She just plumb drove him crazy with her ornery ways."

"Is that true?" The old woman's shoe tapped Lucie's shoe. "Are you a stubborn one?"

Lucie shook her head.

"I reckon you come by it naturally." Lucie looked up at her. "I 'spect she's a lot like me. She even looks like me. You notice that?"

"That's what I always say. Rozella do too. She seem more a Sixkiller 'n a Evers. She got them dark eyes. And she got them Indian ways of yourns. She even gitting your religious ways."

"T'ain't nothing wrong with believing in the good Lord. A soul could do a mite worse, I reckon." A coughing spasm shook her small body. "Dear Lord." She retched up the phlegm and spat. She wiped her mouth with the back of her hand. She looked down at Lucie. "Her father Indian?"

Lucie listened, alert for the answer.

"He musta been." Gracie considered it another moment. "Yes, I think he was."

The old woman leaned over and gave another spit. "I *think* he musta been, too. What color you call that hair?"

"Platinum."

"Sounds like something around your neck. Is Rozella coloring her hair too?"

"Lord knows I've tried. But her hair, ya member how thin and dark it was? It don't take to color same as mine."

"What color you plan to color this child's hair?" Gracie started to protest, but the old woman spoke over her words. "Ya better go on and leave her with me. The next time I see her I might not know her."

Gracie put the grocery bags on the porch, and Lucie followed her out to the Packard. She opened the door and stooped to kiss the child's cheek.

"Now, you be a good girl. Don't go giving your aunt Lizzie any a your trouble. Ya hear?"

Lucie found her mother's slip, running the silky material between her fingers. She leaned into her lap and smelled talcum powder and tobacco. "When ya gonna come back?" she whispered.

The Packard made a U-turn and headed down the road. Lucie saw her mother's hand fly up in a wave, and she returned the wave, her hand flapping high and fast until the car disappeared into the trees. She stood there, watching the clouds of dust settle until there was no sight or sound of her car.

*My momma never said, "I love you." T'wasn't her fault. Indians was just that way. Her momma died when she was three years old, and her daddy didn't hold with that kinda talk. She never heard it, and she never said it to me. You're lucky, people talk 'bout 'em things now.*

*And you Momma? You? But I keep quiet. Hellen, Lizzie, Gracie, and me, not one beggar among us.*

Finally, Lucie turned around and walked up the path to the house, stepping carefully around the vines of peas growing across the path. The old man had disappeared. But, on the top step of the porch, Lizzie stood, her arms crossed around her chest.

She took her position next to the old woman, and they stood side by side, both looking down the road as if expecting Gracie to return.

"Hmpf," the old woman declared, caught the child's eye, and gave a shrug. Then she opened the screen door and went inside the house. Slam, the screen door hit. Lucie sat down on the step, cupped her face in her hands, and fell asleep.

The first night on the farm was passed in restless journeys to and from the bedroom window. She heard Uncle Jerry in the parlor talking to his radio and Lizzie telling him to hush up. The window faced the road, and Lucie watched the light of the moon move over the trees. From a distance the creek ran with the breeze. She pulled the quilt around her and waited at the window. Drifting in and out of sleep, waking with a jerk when she heard a noise, she stayed at her post. The rooster crowed at dawn. She mistook his greeting for the sound of a car and pushed her face up against the window. When it became light outside, she fell into a deep sleep.

She woke to the sound of a door shutting. She heard the screen door hit and the clink of a pail. Lucie spread the quilt on the bed, smoothed the pillows, and looked around for her grocery bags. She had carried them into her bedroom and put them in the corner. The old woman had watched her with the first and followed with the second bag, but Lucie had run and taken it from her. She looked in the other corners of the room, under the bed, but the bags were gone.

She put on her fancy dress and tied the pink ribbon in her hair. Slowly she opened the door and looked around. There wasn't a sound in the house. The kitchen was empty, the old woman's door was closed; carefully, she crept into the parlor. There was an old red sofa, a rocking chair, a wide table with a large Motorola radio on it, and next to the front door, a large bureau stretched across the wall. Everywhere was the color of needle and thread: peacocks strutted across the chair cushion, dainty lace doilies curled around objects on the bureau, and a white cloth with the Lord's Prayer stitched in red and blue hung from the top of the sofa. Yesterday she had not stopped to look around, and now she went to the rocking chair and studied the peacocks, her finger tracing the thread as it fanned into feathers. She turned the knobs on the radio, the big one, then a smaller one, and jumped at its sudden loud buzz. She swung the knob around again and the buzz stopped.

Her eye caught a glint in the room, and she went

to the bureau. There was a small gold box with an Indian woman painted on it. The woman had long black hair and a face like Lizzie's. On either side were photographs of children and old people, in overalls and hats and a jacket. Lucie studied the photographs, wondering who all these people were. In one bent photograph a beautiful dark-haired woman held a baby up to her cheek; she was wearing a plain cotton dress and standing in a field before a wood.

"That there's your momma."

Lucie almost dropped the picture. The old woman came up from behind, replaced the picture on its doilie, and walked back to the kitchen.

She followed her great aunt to the kitchen door, watching as the old woman lit the stove and moved about the kitchen. She took a basket and said, "Come along," and Lucie followed her out the screen door to the chicken coop in back. At the side of the shed the old woman scooped a coffee can into a large feed sack of grain. She handed Lucie the basket, unfastened the wire mesh door, and turned to the child. "Always keep this here door shut."

"Keep 'em wild dogs away, eh, Lizzie?" She heard Uncle Jerry chuckle to himself in the garden.

"Wild dogs?"

"Don't be a-fearing this child none, old man. Sides, they only come round at night, and they only likes chicken dinners."

"They eat the chickens?"

"Ifn they got the chance, they ain't gonna say no. I know I ain't." Uncle Jerry laughed and slapped his leg.

Lucie saw them howling, circling the birds, snapping and dragging the smallest hen into the trees. In the trailer next to Auney's and Uncle Tom's, there had been a dog, a big ugly growling dog that jerked the ends of its chain trying to get at her. She saw the saliva around his mouth and said, "I know a wild dog."

"I don't doubt it. And I spect y'all meet a few more 'fore the good Lord's done with ya." The old woman chatted her way through the chickens, throwing handfuls of grain on the ground. "Here chick chick, here chick chick, here chick." They clucked and ran for the grain, scurrying back to peck at the basket. One mistook one of Lucie's shoes for feed and pecked at it.

"Git away. Make 'im stop!"

"Shoo!" The old woman stamped her foot.

Lucie stamped her foot. "Shoo! Shoo!"

"Ya know better than that, Annabel. I raised ya

with good manners. Now, go on . . . shoo! . . . my, but y'alls pretty today . . . don't step on Campbell, sister, she's an old one and don't move too fast . . . now, where's your egg?"

In the kitchen the old woman cut the biscuits and put a spoonful of bacon grease for the flour gravy in a cast-iron skillet. Carefully, she examined her eggs, placing the largest one on the bread board, and handed the others to Lucie to wrap in rags and put into the carton.

"T'ain't a bad morning. We made ourselves nine cents this morning." Lucie thought about the quarter J. D. had given her and decided, if her Granma let her stay, to give it to the old woman.

Lucie pushed a chair up to the stove to make the gravy.

"What y'all doing with that chair? It's bigger'n yourself."

"I always makes Momma's breakfast," the child said, then added, "I'm a good cook, Momma says."

The child reached for the spoon and started to climb the chair. The old woman studied her for a moment, then clucked and shook her head.

"Flour?" Lucie said, and the old woman pointed to the bin on the stove. She reached over and put her hand in the bin, sprinkling the flour around the grease. When it was paste she called, "Milk?" and the old woman bent down to the milk pail and passed her a dipper. She stirred and stirred, and when it bubbled, she called, "I done cooked it!"

"You're sure 'bout that? What 'bout this here egg?"

"I have a quarter. J. D. give it to me." She stirred and scraped the bottom of the skillet.

"Take that chair away now. Let me finish up here." She took the biscuits out of the oven and dribbled bacon grease over them. Lucie stood by the side of the stove as the old woman put bacon grease in a small skillet and fried the egg. The room was warm and smelled of fresh bread and frying meat. Lucie's mouth watered with the smells, and her stomach growled.

Lizzie opened the screen door and yelled, "Old man. Your biscuits is getting cold." She turned and stumbled into Lucie. "Go on. Sit yourself down. I 'spect you're hungry, going 'out supper last night."

The child climbed a chair and balanced herself on her knees. The old woman looked over at her, went out of the room, and came back with a thick book. It was a well-thumbed dilapidated Bible bound in worn red leather. "I don't think the good Lord would mind," and she placed the book in the seat of the child's chair.

She slipped the egg into the middle of a plate, surrounding it with biscuits and gravy, and placed it in front of the child. Uncle Jerry slipped into the chair next to Lucie and eyed her egg.

"I see ya done got Lizzie to give up one a her eggs."

"Shush up, old man." From the pantry she took out a jar of preserves and Lucie's jar of peanut butter and placed them on the table.

"This here ain't one a your momma's fella's thieving, is it?

Lucie shook her head and said, "It's mine."

"An' it most likely'll stay yours, too. Did your momma think we're so backward here we ain't got peanut butter?" The old woman sat down and bent her head. She lifted her eyes and looked at the biscuit in Lucie's hand. The child put the biscuit down and folded her hands.

"Thank ya, dear Lord, for this here food we's 'bout to eat. And thank ya, dear Lord, for bringing us good health and peace a mind. And thank ya, dear Lord, for allowing this old man and me to see another summer."

Lucie reached for her biscuit, but Lizzie's eyes caught her.

"An' bless this here child, dear Lord. An' help me

and this old man to know how to do the best we can, dear Lord. Amen."

Lizzie sopped a biscuit in gravy. "I unpacked your things this morning," the old woman said between bites, "but I didn't find much that'll be useful here. T'ain't much use for pretty dresses round here."

"My momma bought 'em dresses."

"Your momma has a weakness for pretty dresses. Always has. She minds me a my sister Eveline. Always thinking the next place'll be prettier'n the last one. They running so fast they ain't got time to know who they are."

Lucie glanced down at her pink lap and bent closer over her plate. She soaked the biscuit in the yolk. It tasted of bacon and egg and fresh bread. She missed the smell of coffee and cigarettes and her mother's high running voice. She missed the conspiracy of the morning, J. D. going off to Fort Sill, and her mother coming to the kitchen table. She saw her mother, sitting there alone, with no one to bring her coffee and no one to listen to her.

"I can make coffee," Lucie said.

"I do love a good cup a coffee," Lizzie said, lingering for a moment. "T'ain't no use sitting round here all day. Day's a-wasting, that's for sure."

Lucie followed her to the bureau, where she pulled the bottom drawer open and said, "That there's yours." She had never seen her clothes so neatly folded and organized. In Lawton she kept her clothes in the laundry basket next to her pallet. And it was always a jumble, a grabbing and smelling of this and that. Her great aunt took, from the top, a white shirt and trousers.

"I seed ya know how to dress yourself."

"I been dressing myself a long time."

"Ya a-gonna need some running round shoes. Maybe when we take 'em eggs to town, we'll get ya something ain't afraid a little Oklahoma dust."

She sat on the back porch and watched Lizzie walk to the barn, the pails of slop swinging against her thin legs. At the side of the barn Lizzie stopped and called out, "You be careful with that lye, old man." She saw Uncle Jerry's lips move, but he just kept stirring as if no one had spoken. He was a true Evers, Momma said, as slow as molasses and sweet as pecan pie.

*Thirty years later I remember watching Uncle Jerry and Lizzie negotiate their farming chores. They had a silent choreography of energy and time: Lizzie moved faster and finished by midday, Uncle Jerry drawled through*

89

*the day, coming into the parlor with a slow list of things he was a-fixing to do tomorrow. "All in the good Lord's time," he said before sitting down in his rocker and taking up his pipe. And Lizzie calling from the kitchen, "The good Lord helps those who help theirselves."*

The morning was still cool; a grayness hung over the fields. She sat on the back step and held her legs tightly to her chest. She heard Uncle Jerry's voice from the side of the barn. It was like overhearing a conversation through a thick wall. His mouth moved continuously, but, now and then, he stopped stirring, stared at something in the distance, and said with a shake of his head, "I don't see no sense in it. Lordy, Lordy. I sure don't see no sense. All this pushing and pushing and the mountain's behind ya."

Lucie looked around for the mountain. There was only a little hill to one side of the barn. She heard Momma say, "He ain't right in the head," and saw Auney touch her head and say, "Not right."

Uncle Henry and Uncle Jerry had fought in World War I. Uncle Henry had lost his right leg and, Momma said, Uncle Jerry had lost his peace of mind. He had come back from overseas talking to himself, and Lizzie had kept her promise to marry him. Uncle Henry promised to look after him, and the farmer rented him this little farm outside Davis. Somehow, these two old people had survived the seasons and bad crops and the children that didn't come.

Uncle Jerry came down the yard, lost in his overalls, his lips moving at a steady conversational pace. He tipped his hat and bent to the woodpile, giving his whole attention to the wood for his fire. Lucie picked up a log and followed him. "Mighty kind a ya," he said when she offered her log. She squatted on the bottom rail of the pen. The vapors from the cooking lye made her eyes smart, but she leaned forward into it to escape the rotting pen behind her.

"Mind yourself. I hear tell of a sow over a ways dragged a baby right into her pen." Lucie scooted forward on the rail. "She didn't mean nothing by it, she'd just taken it for her own baby." Lucie stood up and looked through the rails. The baby pigs were round and as cute as pets, but the momma hog was ugly, her snout and face covered with thick short hairs.

"Oink, oink," Lucie called and made a face. The mother hog snorted and looked mean and stupid.

"Don't be unneighborly, Sarah. This here's Gracie girl." The hog turned and stretched out in the mud. "She don't take to strangers. Do ya, girl? Now don't be that way. T'ain't no reason to pout. I ain't gonna hold it against you none . . ."

Lucie drifted into the barn. The smell of manure and hay was sweet and wild. The barn was empty. Outside she discovered a cow tied to a post on the other side of the barn. "Now, don't ya pout," she said as she came up to the cow, "You be a good girl." Lightly she ran her small hand across the cow's flank. The cow shook her head and a bell jangled around her neck. "Now, don't ya pout," she whispered, sneaking up from behind and hitting the bell.

"Moo-oo-oo!" the cow wailed and slapped her tail.

Lucie leaped back. "You be a good girl," she said as she backed away. "Be a good girl."

She bumped into Lizzie. "Put this here kerchief on. The sun'll fry your brains." Lizzie stooped and tied the kerchief around the child's head. "Now stay away from that lye. That old man ain't got your sense."

Lucie sat on the back step and watched Uncle Jerry and Lizzie go about their chores. She curled up in the warm sun and fell asleep. She heard a voice in her ear say, "I too have lived here."

*I too have lived here.*

She woke to Lizzie's voice over her. "Get outta that sun, sister, come on and go with me." She followed the old woman out to the chicken coop. "Ya member what I did this morning?" Lucie nodded. "Let's see if you can take care of these here chickens."

Lucie scooped the coffee can full of grain, spilling some of it as she held it against her chest and stood on tiptoe to unfasten the door. "Here chick chicky, here chicky, here chick," and the birds flocked close around her. "Go over there, over there," she called when they began to peck her shoes, "go on, shoo!" She threw handfuls of feed to them and stamped her foot, "Go on, shoo!"

At supper Lizzie fried bacon and made a pot of grits. Uncle Jerry ate silent but nodding, now and then chuckling to himself. Lizzie heated the water for the dishes. She washed and Lucie dried, getting up and down from her chair at the sink to place each plate and cup back on the table for breakfast. From the parlor came the voices of the radio and Uncle Jerry's replies.

He sat in the rocker with a fresh bulge of tobacco in his cheek, listening and answering with the care of a good host. Lucie sat on the floor between the radio and him. Her mother danced to the radio or laughed or talked over it, oblivious to what the voices might be saying. But Uncle Jerry sat there, intent and polite, giving the voices the courtesy of a good hearing. He believed, Lucie soon discovered, that the voices spoke directly to him and waited for his response. He was a gentle man, unwilling to offend anyone. His replies were courteous and quick, if a little formal.

Lizzie sat opposite on the sofa, holding a flour sack and stretching it this way and that. She cut two sides of it and called, "Sister, c'mon here."

She stood in front of the sofa and Lizzie wrapped the sack around her chest, marked it, and stretched it the length of her arm. "I believe this'll be big enough. For two at least. I'll make one a 'em short sleeve and one a 'em long sleeve for the 'jama top. I'll make 'em a little big so's ya got room . . ."

"Sh-h-h!" Uncle Jerry complained, "The man done ask me a question, and with all this here racket I plumb lost it."

"Foolishness," Lizzie said under her breath and motioned Lucie back to her place.

The child woke with the rooster. She knelt on her pallet at the window and watched the day creep over the tops of the river trees and then across the fields. A mist of light passed in front of the fading moon, and she watched it disappear and then reappear in the sky.

*Look for me in the moon. I'll be watching you from the moon.*

A breeze blew through the window and cooled her face. Lucie pulled the quilt around her. In the distance she heard the creek, water gently washing against rocks and shore. She heard the breeze come rushing through the leaves of the trees and watched as a branch, here and there, swung in the shadows.

Soon she heard Uncle Jerry mumbling through the kitchen, the screen door hit, and his quick steps crossed the backyard to the outhouse. In the next room she heard Lizzie coughing. Lucie smoothed the quilt on the bed and got under it. The cool morning air played at the outside of her cover and she curled under it. The last thing she heard before falling asleep was the screen door hit and Uncle Jerry say, "Mister Coffee, I want to introduce myself."

The child slept on the floor, and Lizzie surprised her one morning. "Y'all catch your death of cold on that there floor." From then on, the sound of Uncle Jerry's mumbling, the screen door hitting, sent her climbing into the bed. Sometimes, before J. D. had moved in, she had slept with her mother or with Auney in the small bedroom, but she had never had a bed of her own. It seemed unnatural to have all that big space to herself. She couldn't get comfortable in that big bed.

The days went on, one after the other. "She'll be good company for ya," her mother had said to Lizzie. But neither the old woman or the child ever sought out company, and as they became more accustomed to the presence of the other, they fell into an understanding of silence and solitude. Uncle Jerry lived on the rim; he was there, always talking and moving slowly from one chore to the next, he deferred to Lizzie, wanting her praise as much as Lucie did, but he was never far from his own voices.

The child was homesick for her mother's talk. She missed her mother's wagging bitter tongue, missed the gossip and laughter, but she drifted into a comfort and freedom with the old people. She thrived in the old woman's watchful silence and found in the old man's preoccupation a way to her own thoughts. Soon she was hearing and conversing with her own voices. Sitting on top of the hill, she played house and told her children stories. She told them about Amos 'n' Andy and the Shadow, and she made up a story about a man who killed all his wives and stuffed them into the closet. She called him Bluebeard.

At first she was confused by the freedom and waited, watching Lizzie's chores closely to be able to repeat them, for the morning when a loud drunken voice demanded she "do her share." She followed the old woman, ready to work and show she was not a lazy and selfish girl. Lizzie tolerated her duckling in the morning, praised her when she finished with the chickens, but when she sat down in the afternoon to her sewing or crocheting, she grew impatient with the child sitting on the floor.

"Go on. Ya gonna have enough time to sit with old women, no need to do it all right this minute."

Lizzie made shirts out of the flour sack and trousers out of the feed sack. Down the length of one arm was stenciled MCCABE'S BAKER'S FLOUR. The trousers were burlap and loose. Lizzie had run a string through the waist to hold them up. The child gave up her Buster Browns and ran barefoot everywhere. Except the outhouse. Then she carefully put on her shoes and tied the shoestrings tight. Uncle Jerry had hammered together a step for her. She pushed it to the toilet, climbed, and rested her feet on it. She tried to sing, like Uncle Jerry, but the place smelled bad so she kept her mouth tightly shut.

"I'm a-going to work," the child began to announce at the end of breakfast. She pushed the egg basket off its nail and opened the screen door wide. Before she got to the chicken coop she was calling, "Here chick chicky, chicky chicky," and the birds flew against the wire mesh trying to get at her. She learned their names and habits, learned how to tease them, pretending to throw a handful of feed and watching them rush, while she stomped her foot and cried, "Shoo! shoo! shoo!"

"You! Sister! Stop tormenting them chickens," Lizzie would yell, and reluctantly the child gathered her eggs and left the hens in peace. But when Lizzie was away from the house, Lucie crept up to the coop and wagged her finger through the wire. They clucked and threatened and pushed to get a bite of her finger. She drove the cow to distraction, sneaking up behind Betsy and slapping her bell. "Leave 'em animals be!" Lizzie yelled across the yard. "You're gonna taint her milk, ifn ya keep at her that way."

When she tired of telling stories and teasing the animals, she took little trips outside the yard. Day by day, she went a little farther from Lizzie's watchfulness. By midsummer she was taking afternoon walks down the dirt road, singing and talking to herself between the trees. One afternoon Uncle Jerry passed her with his fishing pole. She followed him down to the creek. It was smaller than she imagined, sitting in her room and listening to it, and it was still, pretending to be asleep. Uncle Jerry took his seat next to the bank. He dipped a coffee can into the creek and brought it up, the water running out of the holes in the bottom of the can. Inside, Lucie saw, were tiny swimming fish.

"Baby fish," she said.

"Yep. The baby catches the momma."

He took one and strung it through his hook.

"Ugh! Ya gonna kill 'im."

"He don't hardly mind, do ya, Mister Minnow? He was made for swimming near a shore and bringing in a trout. He's happy to be a service."

Uncle Jerry threw his line into the creek.

"Momma says there's witches down there."

"Well, now, that there's a serious charge."

"Ya seen 'em?"

"Once I seen 'em." He took a plug of tobacco out

of his overalls and bit off a piece. He sat patiently, looking over the creek into the trees beyond. Lucie watched his line. "Once when we's still living with Lizzie's folks, a whole gang of 'em witches came banging up the door in a middle a night. They was dressed like ghosts, white sheets all over their-selves. I knew they was witches, and I hightailed it to the back room. Lizzie tried to git me to come out, but I told her, 'I don't want no evil eye.'"

"What happened?"

"What always happens with witches. Mischief. Up to no good."

"What'd they do? They *kill* anybody?"

"Pshaw! They's a lot of screaming an' running round a house. But they can't kill a man. A man's gotta kill hisself."

"They musta wanted something."

"They wanted Frank Sixkiller to sell off his pasture land. And he did too. Didn't wanna lose his only milk cow. They done kilt the first one. He got 'im a lawyer, but that lawyer 'vised 'im to keep outta trouble. One 'em ghosts bought that land, for no money atall." He spat a gob of brown liquid onto the ground and wiped his mouth with the back of his hand. "Looks like all our talk a witches done scared off the fish."

"Momma says the witches live in the bottom of the creek."

"Sh-h-h. There ain't but one witch in this here creek. And that's that smart fish a-laughing at me all these years. Well, your day gonna come, Mister Fish. You just keep a-laughing."

Lucie sat quiet. She leaned over and whispered, "Maybe that fish knows more witches?"

"I wouldn't be none surprised," he whispered. "He might knowed the devil hisself."

Lucie pulled her feet beneath her and said, "Momma says rivers talks."

"Sure they do. No telling what's a-living down there. They's alive just same as you and me."

"And Lizzie."

"Now I wouldna be repeating none a this to Lizzie. She a good woman, ain't no better woman on earth, but she ain't got much foolishness in her."

"I heard the river."

"Did ya now? What did this here creek have to say?"

"I heard it at night when ever body's asleep but 'em wild dogs. Who-oo-oo, I heard 'em wild dogs."

"Was they bothering your chickens?" Uncle Jerry laughed and shook his head.

She drew herself up. "I ain't gonna let 'em a

101

touch my chickens. I chased 'em away. Shoo! I says. Shoo! And they's run away."

The line dipped. Lucie's eyes flew open. "Maybe its them witches," she warned. Uncle Jerry jerked back his pole and the line came up empty.

"Durn, ifn that smart fish didn't take my minnow too. I'm a-gonna git ya one a these days, Mister Fish. Ya can mark my word." He took another minnow from the can and turned to Lucie. "I been after 'im a long time. Listen to 'im, he's a-laughing at me. Sure as we's sitting here, he's a-having hisself a good laugh."

At supper they had ham and hominy. Lizzie looked from one to the other. "I guess that fish outsmarten ya once again, old man?"

"His time's a-coming. The Bible says there's a time fer ever thing. I'm a-waiting on mine."

Uncle Jerry went to his radio, and Lucie sat on the floor between the radio and Lizzie on the couch. The old woman sewed and the old man and child listened for every word from the Motorola. Uncle Jerry advised Amos in his schemes, counseled women in the soap operas, knew a fib when he heard one, believed the Shadow was invincible, and always greeted the Lone Ranger with the same objection. "Now whoever heard a Indian named Tonto?

There's Frank Sixkiller and George Cornsilk and Murray Bell. But I ain't never heard a no Indian named Tonto."

The child thought it over and one night explained, "Maybe he's a old Indian. Like those Indians in the movies?"

The old man thought it over. "Maybe. He musta be from outta state."

*"What's it like being Indian?"*

*I tell them the story of Uncle Jerry and Tonto. The story is dreamed more than known. I hear the voices from the radio and Uncle Jerry's replies. There are parts lost forever and parts true enough to make a life, maybe not a whole life but a decent life.*

Every Saturday Uncle Henry and Aunt Bertha came down the road in their wagon pulled by two slow mules. "These mules are full-blooded Evers," Uncle Henry joked, "they're as slow as molasses and ornery as hell." He hopped down off the wagon, reached up quick as a bird, and snatched his crutch. With another snatch he was carrying a pair of skinned squirrels. Five leaps and he was through the peas, on the front porch, smiling and holding the squirrels out to Lizzie.

"I took a mind to shoot me some squirrels this morning. Durn things beginning to outnumber me and Bertha." He kicked his crutch to the side and sat down. "How're y'all this morning? How's that cough Lizzie? Y'all looking a little peaked."

He was the oldest, named for his father, and he had spent time in the Indian boarding school run by Southern Baptists. But his father had brought him home and put him to work in the fields again, before he could properly read or write. Aunt Bertha was his Choctaw wife. "Think she a thoroughbred living with jackasses," Momma and Auney said. She had a round Indian face and was small and plump like her husband. They had ten children and every one had gone to college.

*"Ever' one," Gracie said. "Just imagine all 'em boys and girls, and ever' one went on to college."*

*"Ever' one," Auney said.*

*"Just imagine all 'em Indian boys and girls going on to college." Her mother wagged her finger at Lucie. "There ain't many Indians go on to college."*

*"There surely ain't."*

They worked a small piece of land just beyond the river. They had a little tar-roofed shack at the edge of the land. After the seventh child, Uncle Henry had found a round silver trailer and pulled it up behind the shack. He and Aunt Bertha moved into the shack, with the baby, and left the other kids in the shack. The kids were gone, but they still lived in the trailer, using the shack only for cooking and company.

"Ready when you are," Uncle Henry called through the screen.

"I'll only be a minute," Lizzie called back.

His merry eyes settled on Lucie. "You're Gracie's little girl. I coulda told any body that. Ya look just like your momma when she's a girl. Ya just as wild?"

Lizzie said behind her, "I think she looks more'n like Helen. She's got those same eyes and quiet ways."

"She's pretty, same as Helen," Aunt Bertha added.

"Say what ya like 'bout half-breeds, they sure do make pretty children. Ya coming in to town with us? In that pretty pink dress?" Lucie grinned. "I'm afeared I might shame ya in my old overalls," he said, and hopped up, grabbing his crutch in an instant. He pointed the crutch at Uncle Jerry. "How long's it been since ya seen our Sarah? She coming in with her two boys next week, and I'm fixing to butcher that big hog a mine. Y'all come on over, and we'll have us a to do. Ya can help yourself to some a that hog. There's enough for twenty families."

"Thank ya. Right kindly." Uncle Jerry was nodding away. "Yep, right kindly."

Uncle Henry scooped Lucie into the back of the wagon, and Lizzie handed the egg basket to the child and climbed up next to Bertha. She took the basket onto her lap and told the child to hold tight. From the porch Uncle Jerry waved, already, Lucie thought, on his way to the river. The wagon bumped along the main road, pulling over a few times to let cars pass.

"Go on," Uncle Henry waved them by, "I ain't going no place in a hurry."

When they came to town Uncle Henry pulled to the side of the road and waited. "Make sure ya git them two biddies to git ya a piece a candy, hear?" he called out as Lucie passed him.

Davis was a few wooden buildings, a general store with a bus stop in front, and the Shack, a restaurant specializing in breakfast and lunch. Inside, dozens of white farmers milled around, sitting on stools at the counter or standing in place, drinking coffee and smoking cigarettes. Aunt Bertha and Lizzie walked past with their heads down and

106

turned away. Lucie hesitated at the window and two farmers looked up and waved to her. Lucie smiled and waved.

"Don't go encouraging 'em," Lizzie said, taking her arm. "That ain't no place for us."

"Why?" Her momma had worked in Lawton's Chicken Shack. Sometimes her mother came home with fried chicken stuffed in her purse; sometimes she hid a piece of pie underneath the chicken. And they stayed up late, wiping their greasy hands on their clothes, licking the pie from their fingers, and Momma telling stories about the "good ol' boys" at the shack.

"Why?" Lizzie asked, incredulous. She caught the child by the hand and they walked a space before the old woman turned and said, "Why? You're different, that's why."

The child thought a moment and asked, "Why?"

"Lordy, you're too little to have all these questions."

"That's just when they do have 'em," Aunt Bertha said.

"Why?" She handed the egg basket to Bertha and bent down. "There ain't no why 'bout it. You're just different." She stood up but kept the child by the hand. "Sister, I don't mean to be mean, but

107

people who ask a lot of whys usually end up with hard lives. Ya listening?"

When they returned to Uncle Henry and the wagon, Lucie had a fistful of penny candy. Lizzie had given her a nickel from the eggs, and she had walked from jar to jar, looking but not asking, and finally, when the clerk stood above her, she held up her nickel and pointed to the jars with red candies. Behind the wagon's seat, she uncurled her fingers and showed Uncle Henry. He laughed and told her to hold tight. She put her candies on her lap and admired them. The best one was a large red jaw-breaker. It was for Uncle Jerry.

One morning, well into midsummer, Lucie appeared at the kitchen table and sat down. An especially humid night still hung heavy in the morning, but the child sat on her Bible shivering.

"Ya cold, sister?" Lucie shook her head. "I'm surprised ya ain't pushing some chair up to this here stove. Who's gonna make my gravy? Lord knows I'm happy enough to give my hand to it with you outta the way. Maybe ya feel like a little grits?"

Lizzie sat a bowl of grits in front of the child and waited. Listlessly, the child watched the butter melt on the grits, then brought a few spoonfuls up to her mouth, but could do no more than look at it before returning it to the bowl.

"Maybe she want a biscuit," Uncle Jerry suggested.

Lizzie halved a biscuit, smeared it generously with peanut butter and honey, and placed it on the table in front of the child. Lucie nibbled the biscuit, licked the peanut butter and honey, then put it down on her plate. The old woman reached her long thin arm across to her forehead.

"A fever, a mite high. Looks like youse a mite sick, sister."

She stripped the sheets and pillowcases on the bed, helped her into clean trousers and shirt, as if the offending germ might be rooted out by a healthy dose of soap and water and an old-fashioned scrub. When she pulled the quilt up to Lucie's chest, she almost bent to kiss her cheek, but she collected herself, taking up the bundle of dirty clothes and calling from the door, "I told ya not to go a-sleeping on that there floor. Now ya gonna have to learn the hard way, I guess. Don't ya move, ya hear?"

The child slept, a warm and fitful sleep, waking in a clammy sweat. She pulled her eyes open and a cold cloth was pressed against her forehead. The old woman sat in a kitchen chair close to the bed. She saw a shadow leave the doorway.

A bright summer sun came through her window. She kicked the covers off and felt them being tucked tightly around her. There was the sound of whispers, shadows moving close to her bed, the smell of sage burning. She pushed to the surface and saw a dark little woman, in a red shawl and pumpkin beads, standing over her with a drum and singing the same phrase again and again in a foreign tongue.

*To tsu hwa ha tlv we da, to tsu hwa ha tlv we da, to tsu hwa ha tlv we da, to tsu hwa tlv we da, to tsu hwa tlv we da.*

From a dream the little woman bent down to her and said, "Redbird, where have you been?" She started to say she had been on the moon, but the bed was warm and soft, the air was sleepy. Then the darkness came, and she walked out of the room on the bright beams of a full round moon. "Wait," she called to the little woman ahead of her, surefooted and quick on the light, her red shawl balancing the heavens. "Wait," she called again. The woman turned and said with resignation, "Don't hurry. Your time comes fast."

From another place she heard chickens squawk and the howl of circling wild dogs. She saw herself running, circling the chicken coop, and yelling, "Shoo! Shoo! Go on!"

"Sister, you're dreaming."

"'Em wild dogs . . . shoo!"

"Sugar, ain't no body bothering your chickens."

"Shoo! Shoo!" She tried to run faster, but there was a weight against her. Then she was in her bed, listening and watching, trying to remember where she was and where she had been. She heard coughing, a reaching deep into the lungs, heard someone spit into the coffee can, and waited for Lizzie's sigh and the words, "Dear God." She heard the cough, the sigh, the words every night, but now, listening through the fever, she knew Lizzie was sick.

"Poor Lizzie," the child said and tried to touch the old woman.

"I thought ya were worried 'bout your chickens?"

From the back of the house came the sounds of Uncle Jerry chasing and clapping his hands. "Shoo! Shoo!" he shouted. "Go on, ya varmints, don't let me see ya round here again."

She felt the washcloth wet on her face, and she

111

heard Lizzie say, "Ya see, the old man's a-watching out for your chickens." She closed her eyes and fell into the warm darkness again.

*She was running, running fast down the dirt road. She was wearing her pink dress and red cowboy boots. She came up behind Uncle Henry in his wagon, and he pulled over and let her pass. She looked around her. Momma was driving with Auney and Uncle Jerry next to her. Uncle Henry was hopping next to her. "Run," he shouted, "don't let 'em dogs git a hold a your leg." She heard the dogs coming over the river, yapping and tearing through the trees. She saw the main road just ahead, but it kept slipping away, and the dogs were on either side of her, coming through the woods. A small woman with a long black braid stood at the end of the road. "Hey," she yelled, but the woman didn't turn around. "Help! Help!" she screamed, but knew no words left her mouth. "Help! Help!" The woman turned around. Her Indian face was blank and uninviting. Slowly she said, "C'mon, ifn ya coming." Lucie ran for her, almost touching her red shawl before slipping back down the dirt road. Again and again she tried to reach her, but the distance wouldn't close. She heard the dogs and felt them yapping at the hem of her dress and she began to scream . . .*

"It's just the fever," a woman's voice said over her. She felt arms around her and, for a moment, believed she had reached the woman. The arms lifted her and carried her into the parlor. Lizzie held her close, rocking her back and forth in the rocker. Lucie snuggled against her chest and whimpered. She heard the old woman say, "Ain't nothing to fret about. I ain't gonna let 'em spirits steal ya away. Don't ya fret none. I ain't a-gonna let nothing happen."

She woke with the morning sun on her face. Next to her, Lizzie slept. The coughing had awakened her once or twice during the night. She remembered Lizzie's sigh, "Dear God," the old woman getting up, the sounds of crying from the parlor (perhaps it was the sounds of her own crying she remembered?), and the old woman lying down again. Slowly she scooted to the edge of the bed.

"Where y'all going?" Lizzie was sitting up in bed. She had a bobby pin in her mouth, already rearranging the pins into a tight bun. "Ya stay right where ya are. Ya need bed rest for a couple a days, hear?" She smoothed the quilt up to the child's chin and went into the kitchen.

Uncle Jerry appeared with a cup of herbal tea. It tasted bitter, and Lucie took tiny sips, struggling to swallow the foul liquid. He returned with a cup of hot water and molasses. "This here'll taste a mite better, I reckon." But it was hot and too sugary, and she snapped her mouth shut. He pulled a spoon out of his overalls pocket.

"The old woman thought ya might need this." He offered her a spoonful of water. "She said you're to take all a this."

He offered her another spoonful. "Ya hear any more from 'em wild dogs?"

"I dreamt 'em." She became animated, "They was a-chasing me through the trees and I was running fast but I . . . I saw Grandma last night."

"Hellen? Ya saw Hellen?" The name was said quietly, with the regret of a first love. It was spoken so that the word carried a small gentle image.

"I saw her. At the end of the road. She said, 'C'mon, ifn you're a-coming.'"

"She was a-waiting for ya. In case ya passed over." He thought a moment. "Hellen was always a kindly person. She took care a them girls till she couldn't no more."

Lucie took another spoonful. "How come she didn't live with you and Aunt Lizzie? It's nice here. I bet she woulda liked it."

Uncle Jerry addressed someone else in the room.

114

"She wanna know how come ya didn't live here." He paused, listening to the other side of the argument, and finally said, "There ain't no need to go into all that."

"She looked sad."

"I 'spect she is. It's real hard to leave this world when ya got family a-needing ya." He held the spoon to her mouth and smiled. "I seen her myself not too long ago. I smelled sage burning and I looked up, and ifn it weren't Hellen come to say hello. I asked her if I could do something for her, but she just stood there, with that long braid down her back. She were always quiet, wouldn't take nothing from no body. She had more pride than a body need on this earth."

"Was she little, like us?"

"Most Cherokees is little. We's small in body and large in the heart. Your momma tell ya 'bout your people? She teach ya to know who ya are?"

"She says we's Indian."

"Well, now, there's Indians and there's Indians." He looked over in the corner of the room and listened. "When I was in the army, I was that 'little Injun.' Those fellas had seen a whole lotta movies, and they thought Indians could walk and talk without making no noise. Ever' time we come in to a new place a-fighting, they's always talking 'bout 'send that little Injun in first.' That's how your Uncle Henry lost his leg, and I . . . well, I just made it home."

The coughing, the sigh, "Dear Lord," came from the kitchen.

"Momma and Auney says ya lost your mind."

Uncle Jerry laughed, slapping his leg so hard the molasses water spilled on the quilt. "Now ifn that don't beat all! Outta the mouths a babes!"

"I didn't tell ya to wear the child out, old man," Lizzie called from the kitchen.

Lucie whispered, "Did ya lose it?"

He chuckled and said in low voice, "I 'spect I have. After I come back I have a lot more respect for meanness. I listen real hard, and I try to catch it."

"Is there witches in the radio?"

"Sometimes they try to come through the radio, but I don't pay 'em no mind. Mostly, that's just conversing, man to man." He studied on it a moment and grinned. "I git tired all these white voices talking, and I try to give 'em the Indian point of view. Like my daddy woulda done. Just the other day, this man in the radio talking 'bout how this here Eisenhower's a great chief. Shoot! I put 'im straight right away. 'Ain't ya ever heard a Quanah Parker?' I asks. He didn't know what to say."

116

Lizzie came into the room. "That's enough, old man. The youngun gotta sleep. She can't be bothered by your jawing all day. Go on now. Ya think 'em hogs gonna wait till Judgment Day? They ain't got the confidence."

Lucie lay in the bed for two days, sleeping and listening to the sounds of life going on around the farm. Life came to her in the smallest of sounds. Outside, in the bed of peas, she listened to two cardinals exchanging lives. *Redbird, where have you been?* She heard Betsy in the distance, her bell jangling every time she moved. And she followed Uncle Jerry and Lizzie around by their voices, the old woman directing and Uncle Jerry saying, "A body can't do it all in one day."

At night Lizzie climbed into bed next to her, and Lucie lay awake listening to the river and the sound of the breeze through the trees. She pretended to be asleep when Lizzie's coughing took hold and drove her into the parlor. She waited for the sounds of crying, but she heard only the swing of the rocking chair. When Lizzie returned to bed and wrapped her arms around the child, she never moved a muscle.

In the middle of the week the night breeze picked up and the trees whistled. Lucie heard thunder roll and snap in the distance. She listened as the rain came over the fields, fast and heavy, the thunder followed loud and furious, and the lightning turned the night bright. Lizzie got up and closed the window.

"We don't want no lightning a-coming through the window." She made her way around the house, shutting doors and slamming windows. The screen door hit, and Lucie listened to her run to the barn. Uncle Jerry snored in the next room.

*"Let's see if ya can take care a these chickens."*

She jumped out of the bed and flew through the screen door. Her chickens were sitting inside the shed, looking at her like she had no sense. She wagged a finger at them. "Now y'all stay right there. Less ya a mind to be a hit by lightning." A few hens clucked and strutted on their perch, fluffing their dry feathers.

"Lord a mercy!" she heard Lizzie shout behind her, "what're ya doing out here? It's pouring wet!"

The old woman hurried her into the house, lit the stove, and made her sit in front of it with her feet in a basin of hot water. "Ya don't have to worry none 'bout 'em chickens. They's knows better'n you to stay inside in pouring rain."

"I was worring 'bout 'em."

Lizzie leaned into a long hacking cough. The spasm seized and held her until she heaved for breath. She reached across for Uncle Jerry's coffee can and spit into it. "Dear Lord in heaven. I can't figure this here cough."

She poured herself a cup of coffee and sat at the table. "Ya got to learn to worry 'bout yourself." She motioned to Lucie to keep her feet in the water. "Your grandma had the same ways. She always thinking 'bout some body sides herself. And when the time come, she too weak to fight. She passed over real quick. We didn't know nothing till one 'em Jeeter boys come knocking on our door."

"Did ya know my grandma a long time?"

"We was girls together. She the only girl, and she used to come a-visiting me and my sisters. We knowed her long before she got herself in trouble."

"Was she a bad girl?"

"It wasn't no bad 'bout it, it was just trouble. Trouble can find any body. Ya member that. Ya don't have to go looking for it. Ya can be sitting right here minding your own business and trouble can come knocking right at that door."

"Like 'em witches in the creek?"

"Now, there's a lot of Indians believe in the evil eye and witches. I just think it's another name for trouble, myself. Emmie, my own sister, don't go no place 'out her medicine stones. She always got that crystal close to her. Says it protects her. I says she protecting it. But that don't matter. Ya getting warm by that stove?"

She tested the water with her hand and poured some more hot water over the child's feet. Lizzie took a biscuit out of the tin, spread it with peanut butter, and handed it to Lucie.

"Ya want some milk with that?"

Lucie shook her head and asked, "Was Grandma in trouble?"

"Your grandma was the sweetest girl I know. We all lived up there in Stilwell. The Sixkillers. The Evers. The Fields. All lived up there in a settlement. Each of us had our own land. It wasn't good land, but it was passable. Dear Lord, how things have changed." A spasm shook her. She spat into the coffee can and wiped her mouth with her sleeve. She stared at the stains on her sleeve as if she were trying to recognize them.

The thunder and lightning passed, and the rain could be heard tapping against the roof. The child soaked her feet, and the old woman sipped her coffee. Lucie sat quiet and still; she knew you had to wait for a story. Sometimes, she learned later, the waiting is the story.

"I believe some of the Fields still live around Stilwell. Now there's some fellas ya don't wanna run into. Leastways, not when they's drinking. I heard when Gabby Fields died one of his boys took over the land. The rest of us got married and picked some cotton. Ended up renting a piece of land ya ain't meant to make a decent living from. But we still living, I guess that's more'n most bodies."

She noticed the child. "Ya ready for bed?"

Lucie shook her head. She loved the sound of voices talking to themselves. She was a child, small for her age, and adults felt they could say anything to her. True, she didn't understand many of the things said, but she did understand the wish in the voice. And what they might have been and what she could have been was present, for a moment, in the lilt of this wish. When her momma talked to herself or to Auney the hard loudness disappeared and a softness entered her eyes and voice. Sometimes, when Gracie couldn't believe in her stories, she drank; then the stories became quarrels, betrayals carried on behind bathroom doors.

"My feet are cold," she said to Lizzie. The old

woman got up and dipped a cup of hot water into the basin. "Maybe ya need to put your feet in hot water?"

"I'm just fine. Don't ya worry none," Lizzie said and cleared the phlegm from her throat and spit into the coffee can.

"Maybe ya need a doctor?"

"Maybe ya need to stop being so nosy."

"Momma says you're an uppity Indian." She looked down and splashed the water a little.

"I knowed your momma a long time. I pretty much figured out what she think and don't think of me." She paused and listened. "They ain't nothing more satisfying 'n rain on a roof. Listen how it talks, like it's asking to come in." Lizzie put another log in the stove. "I ain't gonna say I approve of your momma's ways. I weren't raised thataway. And your grandma weren't raised thataway. Always dancing and drinking and going around with soldiers. Leaving their families and hightailing it to the cities. It seems like we lost a whole generation of children.

"The Cherokee always been a proud people. They took care of their children and families. That always come first. When my grandaddy come from Georgia he didn't leave no body behind. Nowadays seems like people forget how to look out for their

122

families. But it ain't their fault, I reckon. Times is different. No truer word been said. Now, you're gonna grow up 'out knowing your people. We's not always gonna be round, and ya gonna have to count on your momma. And she can't count on herself. Why she color her hair that yellow color?"

Lucie shrugged. "It makes her look pretty."

"Pretty, my eye. It makes her look like she don't know where she come from. Ya can't make a silk purse out a sow's ear. Member that. The Good Lord give us our coloring. It's his sign to us of where we come from. Ya can't meddle with that 'out meddling with family. Nowadays people believe if they believe it, it makes it so. They forget they're Indian. They forget their white daddies gone off and left 'em 'out a nickel to call their own. They member they's Indian when they need help, ya better believe it. Ain't nothing like trouble to help a person member."

"Did Grandma member? When the trouble come?"

"Shoot! Weren't nothing to member. She knew who she was." She seemed to leave the room for a moment. Lucie could tell she had forgotten the rain. "You's young, but I reckon ya ain't gonna hear it from no body but me. Maybe someday y'all member it and put it in a story. Like 'em books yer Uncle Henry has from the seminary. How's that water a-doing? We'll heat up some more water and this here coffee too. Don't look like no body gonna get much sleep tonight."

Department of the Interior
Commission of the Five Civilized Tribes
Claremore, Indian Territory
November 10th, 1900

In the matter of the application of Robert H. Evers, for the enrollment of himself and children as Cherokee citizens. He being sworn testified before Col. T. B. Needles as follows:

Q: What is your name?
A: Robert Henry Evers.
Q: What is your age?
A: 33.
Q: What is your post office address?
A: Stilwell.
Q: What district do you live in?
A: Cooweescoowee.
Q: Are you a citizen of the Cherokee Nation?
A: Yes, sir.
Q: By blood?
A: Yes, sir.

Q: What degree of blood?

A: Full-blood.

Q: Who do you want to have enrolled?

A: Myself and my children.

Q: Is your wife alive?

A: No, sir.

Q: What is her name?

A: Ada June Evers.

Q: Do you have proof of marriage to her?

A: Yes, sir.

Applicant presents a certificate of marriage certifying that he was married to Ada J. Peebles, a citizen of the United States, on the 1st of November 1883.

Q: What are the names of your children?

A: Henry L.

Q: How old is Henry L?

A: 13.

Q: Next one.

A: Matthew A.

Q: How old?

A: 12.

Q: Next one.

A: Jerry C.

Q. How old?

A: 10.

Q: Next one.

A: Williard.

Q: How old?

A: 8.

Q: Next one.

A: Hellen.

Q: How old?

A: 3.

Q: Next one.

A: That's all.

Q: By what right do you claim citizenship?

A: I have a certificate of admission.

Applicant presents certificate of admission to Cherokee citizenship issued October 18th, 1887, signed by D. W. Lipe, Acting Chairman of the Commission, attested by Henry Hifert, clerk, approved and endorsed by D. W. Bushyhead, Principal Chief, certifying that Robert H. Evers, aged 21 years, was admitted to Cherokee citizenship on the 18th of October 1887.

Q: Are you the identical Robert H. Evers mentioned in this certificate?

A: Yes, sir.

By Cherokee Representative Hastings:

Q: Where were you married?

A: In Georgia.

Q: Where are your children living now?

A: All of them except one live in Georgia. Henry L. is here with me, he has been here only two months.

Q: Have they always lived in Georgia?

A: Yes, sir.

Q: How long have you been here?

A: Since 1894.

Q: Continuously?

A: Yes, sir.

Q: Who are the children living with in Georgia?

A: My mother.

Q: Was there any intention to separate with your wife?

A: No, sir. I always expected her to join me.

Q: Why did she remain in Georgia?

A: It wasn't through no fault of mine. When I come out here her mother was very sick, she is an invalid, in fact, and did not want her to go out here and leave her alone, and she was unwilling to come under these circumstances.

Q: When did your wife die?

A: Two months ago.

Q: Then there was no actual separation between you and your wife?

A: No, sir.

Q: So there were no intentions for a divorce?

A: No, sir.

Q: Would you say you were happy together?

A: Yes, sir. Same as most folks.

Q: Are your children planning to join you?

A: Yes, sir.

By the Commission:

Q: Are you or have you ever been a member of the Ketoowah Society?

A: No, sir.

Q: Have you ever been a party to discussions about seceding from the Union?

A: No, sir.

Q: Would you support the Cherokee Nation in its secession from the Union?

A: No, sir.

Q: Is it your intention to raise your children as citizens of the United States?

A: Yes, sir.

Q: Why have you petitioned for an allotment of land?

A: To find some way of living, sir. For myself and my children.

Q: Do you understand the terms of this allotment?

A: Yes, sir.

Q: Do you understand that said allotment is given to you in trust? That you may not sell or dispose of said allotment? That said allotment may be revoked at the pleasure of this court?

A: Sir?

"HERE, put this here quilt round ya. It's a shame going to bed with this rain tapping on the roof. A body do dream better in a rainstorm. Somehow it lifts a body outta hisself."

She brought the phlegm up from her chest and spit into the coffee can.

"My momma used to say, a story told in the rain brings no tears. I don't know 'bout that. There's been plenty tears shed and a few more wouldna hurt no body. Ya wants to know 'bout trouble. For that ya don't have to go back no further'n tomorrow, but this here trouble starts a long time ago. Before your momma was your age, before your grandma was your age, way back when Oklahoma was Indian Territory."

Lucie saw the long stretch of horizon, the blue sky coming right down to it, and she saw hundreds of thousands of Indians walking across that horizon, each finding his own little piece of rich red earth.

"Was the Indians rich?"

The old woman laughed, slapping her leg and laughing so hard she choked. "Sister, how many rich Indians ya know?"

The child screwed her face up in earnestness. "My momma said Cherokees was rich. They owned niggers and had big farms."

"They weren't none of ours. I heard tell of 'em Cherokees, but I ain't knowed a Indian had two nickels to rub together. Naw, that's another story. This here story's 'bout plain folks just trying to get through this here life 'out more'n their share of trouble.

"I knowed your great-grandaddy. Your great-grandma passed over 'fore she made it to Indian Territory. Name a Ada June, she was a half-breed from 'em Georgia hills. I don't know much 'bout her. Henry and Jerry, they's member. Her daddy were a missionary from up north, and he come down to Rossville to work with the Cherokee. He married a Cherokee woman. Julia, I think her name was. They say your grandma's daddy didn't like her marrying Robert Henry. And I reckon Robert Henry had his own worries, once he start living with her. I hear she 'bout drove him crazy with her holy ways. He weren't a complaining man, but I knowed a few things."

*This is what the old people told me.*

"When my pa first met Robert Henry he had just

come from Georgia. He come by foot, a-picking cotton along the way and eating when he had the chance. He come to my grandparents' home, just this side of Stilwell, and they let him go on and sleep in the barn while he looked for work.

"He were a farmer back home in Georgia, and he got hisself a job working the fields for the Cornsilks. They paid him a dollar a week, dinner, and all the corn he could carry from that there field. We didn't have much, and he didn't wanna take the little we had. He ate a lot of corn during those months. My daddy was a young man, still a-living with his parents. He'd go out to the barn now and then, to share a bottle of corn liquor. Most evenings Robert Henry was right there in his corner, roasting an ear of corn.

"He came to Indian Territory to join up with the Western Cherokee and get his allotment of land. My daddy said he loved to talk about having his own piece of land, and when they had got clean through a bottle of corn liquor, he talked like he had been living on that land for some years. Already had it seeded, planted, and harvested. He had even given it a name: 4 Evers, after his four sons. My daddy didn't hold with breaking up Cherokee land. He said that was the fastest way to destroying the nation, and he was right. Durn right. They almost come to fighting it out a number of times. Robert Henry wanted his own land so bad, he didn't know how to dream another dream."

"How do ya dream another dream?" the child asked. She would change dreams the next the time the wild dogs chased her down the road.

"That's a good question, sister." The old woman sipped her coffee and studied it a moment. "Truth is, I don't rightly know. I reckon most folks is lucky if they got one dream. I ain't never been good at dreaming, myself. I leave all that to the old man."

"Robert Henry, my grandma's daddy, he knowed how to dream."

"Lordy, he sure did. That man saved his money and buried it in the ground in a can. Couple of times a year, when the farm work was slow, he'd a-work his way back to Georgia to see his wife and children. He took his can with him and give all the money to Ada June. He said she kept it in the family Bible, right behind the names of the children. It was during one of his trips Ada June was taken with your grandma. He didn't know nothing about it, but, the next time he come to Rossville, Ada June were a-sitting up with a little baby girl.

"From the day she was born, they all was plumb

crazy 'bout that little girl. Robert Henry give her the name Hellen because the white farmer he sometime work for had a little girl name of Hellen. He said it made him feel good, when he was a ways from his family, to hear the name Hellen called out. After Ada June died, ya never saw Robert Henry or one of 'em boys 'out that little girl perched somewheres on 'em.

"The government give him his allotment in the northwest corner of our land. He sent for Henry, and the two of 'em worked that land from sunup to sundown. The settlement got together and helped 'em put up a little log house. The women got together and stuffed mattresses and pillows and sewed quilts. By the time the other younguns arrived, the house was ready for 'em. They had two rooms. Robert Henry and the boys slept in one and the little girl slept in the other.

"My daddy said Robert Henry was the hardest-working man he ever saw. He went right from the fields to his bed. He nearly worked Henry to death. He knowed what his own land would do, and he was determined to turn that red clay green. Till the day he died, Robert Henry tried to make that land his own. But the land, it grew what it wanted to grow. And mostly that was weeds and notes from the bank.

135

"From the time your grandma was a baby, Robert Henry had his mind set on her becoming a teacher. He didn't read or write, his wife did all his reading and writing for him in Georgia. My daddy said he went right from dreaming 'bout getting his own piece of land to believing his little girl done graduated from the Cherokee Female Seminary up in Tahlequah. He beat his boys something awful, but he never raised his voice to that little girl. If he passed you a-coming out a store, he spent half an hour a-chewing your ear off about his girl. It's a shame, really. Henry was the reader in the family. His momma taught him to read and write a little, and if Robert Henry had allowed him to stay on at the seminary, he would have made a right good teacher."

"How's that water? Would ya like of sip this here coffee?"

Lucie took the old woman's cup and sipped. It tasted foul, like water gone bad, but she took another sip before passing it back to Lizzie.

"Momma says Uncle Henry's uppity."

"Your momma's right fond of that word, I reckon. I ain't saying your momma's wrong. Way I see it, she don't know the story."

136

"You knowed the story."

"Lordy, I couldna help but knowed it. We was like family, and a body's gotta know family."

"Ever' day your great-grandpa sent your grandma over to our house. My momma was supposed to teach her how to sew and cook and keep a house. She were just a slip of a thing, she were littlier than you, with a big moon face and dark eyes. I was two years older'n her and spent most of my days raising hell with Emmie, but your grandma would never join in with us. Her daddy dropped her at our door in the morning, and she was my momma's shadow until he came and picked her up in the evening. To tell the truth, Emmie and I didn't much like her then. Our momma was always a-asking us, 'Why can't you try an' be more like Hellen?' It got so we made a game of it, one of us saying, 'Poor little motherless girl,' and the other 'bout falling on the ground with the giggles.

"Once she surprised us. Old man Cornsilk used to grow the best watermelons in the county. Those melons got as big as a small child, and they just ran with the sweetest juice, dripping down your mouth an' all over your clothes. On hot days Emmie and me would sneak over to his patch and steal us a

137

melon. We'd take it up to the little hill 'hind his house, throw it up against the tree, and sit there eating melon and spitting seeds till we was sick of melon. We musta done it one too many times, cause old man Cornsilk began to 'spect some body was stealing his melons. He took to a-waiting for the thieves, and the next time Emmie and me paid that patch a visit, we found ourselves outrunning buck-shot."

"Did he shoot ya?"

"Naw, child. But it weren't for lack a trying. He a had more luck shooting jackrabbits. Emmie and me hightailed it back up that hill quicker'n the devil at a church meeting." A spasm shook the old woman, and the child watched as she retched the phlegm up and spit it into the coffee can. "Dear Lord," she said and took a sip of coffee. "I guess my troublemaking days is over. I wished I a knowed then how much fun they's gonna be."

"Emmie and me missed those melons some-thing turrible. One day, towards the end of sum-mer, it was awful hot, the sun didn't have nothing to do but make a body miserable. It were too hot for being inside the house, and your grandma took off with us. Emmie and me, our mouths was watering

138

for one a old man Cornsilk's melons, but he scared us real good. We walked over to that there hill and sat under that tree a-looking down at his patch, a-watching his house, and a-trying to get up the courage to go on down and snatch us a melon. All a sudden your grandma stands up and says, 'I'll get ya one of them melons.' And she was down that hill and back with a big old melon 'fore we could say Jack Robinson. I had a number of melons since then, but that was the best-tasting melon I ever ate. We sat under that tree, with its sweet juice a-running all over us, and almost a died laughing when old man Cornsilk came out and shook his fist up at us."

*I saw her running down that hill, her braids flying, the blur of a little body . . . snatch . . . the brown round face running up that hill, the green child tight in her arms, quick as a brave.*

"My momma learned your grandma to cook and bake. She didn't have no luck with Emmie and me. The old man," she pointed to their bedroom, "says I shoulda learned what my momma had to teach me. I says, ya ain't never a-gonna know what ya need till the time's on ya. Emmie and me was right happy 'out a-knowing. When we's wanted a pie or a cobbler for supper, we'd just go out and get your grandma the berries, and she was always willing to oblige us. We used to crave her blackberry pie, and we woulda had it ever' day if momma been willing to spare the sugar.

"Momma petted her, same as Robert Henry and the boys. When she sewed dresses for Emmie and me, she used the leftovers to make a dress for Hellen. She took the girl aside, when the time come, and told her all 'bout the changes of life. Showed her, like she done showed Emmie and me, how to make the rags and wash 'em out. Told her, like she done told us, she was a woman now, and if she slept with a man, she would have his baby. Hellen asked her, as innocent as a child, did this mean her brothers too?

"And Hellen loved my momma, called her Auntie and hung onto ever' word. My momma was good at remembering. When she was a-shelling peas or husking corn, my momma'd sit at the table and member the old people. Her folks and my daddy's folks, all the old people we didn't member or never met. And she membered stories her momma told her. She talked 'bout Georgia and John Ross and her Uncle Mervin, he fought in A Company in the War

140

between the States. She never could member just which side he was on. She talked about her grandma and grandpa, jist like it were yesterday and she just left their house, how they come to Indian Territory with nothing more'n their backs could carry, and how her momma walked straight across the territory, stopping ever' so often to ask where the Cherokee had gone, to find her parents."

*She wanted us to member too, and I guess that's what I'm a-doing with you. History ain't nothing more'n membering. A man can't know who he is all by hisself. A woman neither. Both need something to member.*

"Hellen never got her fill of the old people. She would ask, again and again, when Emmie and me was plain tired of membering, to hear the story one more time. She wanted to hear how Robert Henry had come and lived in my grandaddy's barn and how he had buried his money and how he had borrowed their best mules and wagon to go and get his children. She were a lot like you, always a-wanting to know why this and why that. It got so's Emmie and I just roll our eyes when she started asking her questions. Mostly, though, she listened to my momma, just like a small and quiet little mouse, and all the time ya see her little lips moving like she were a-helping my momma to tell the story.

"But her favorite story, the story she coulda told as good as my momma, was the story 'bout Quanah Parker. Ya heard 'bout him? He was the Indian Jesse James. He were a half-breed, his daddy was a Comanche and his momma a white woman. And if ya were a white settler, a-squatting on Indian lands, ya didn't wanna wake up in the middle of the night an' find him standing right over your bed. Lordy, no, that woulda been your worst nightmare.

"Him and his renegades'd ride down from them hills and kill them white settlers, women and children too. Indians say it was the white blood made him so mean. It wasn't right, killing those women and children. But I says it were the circumstances. A man can only be as good as his time allows him to be.

"My momma met him. She was only a child at the time, but she membered how he rode up, with his half-breed renegades, right into the middle of their yard. The soldiers were a-looking for him, and it was dangerous to be anywhere near him in those days. But he rode right up into their yard, and her momma and aunties killed almost all their chickens to feed him and those renegades. 'Lord have mercy,' they all said, running in circles, 'it's Quanah Parker hisself.' They put him and his Indians up in the barn for the night. All night her momma and aunties stood guard outside that barn. When he left the next morning, her momma and aunties gave 'em water and packed food bags for 'em to take. All those women and children collected in the yard and watched 'im take off for the hills again. When their men come back, they told 'em, and my momma's daddy figured Quanah Parker had knowed Indian women and children needed his protection."

"Was he handsome?" the child asked.

"Sister," the old woman said, "handsome weren't the word for it. The man was so pretty he had to get hisself a mansion to hold all his wives. And still had to do some more building."

"The sound of that rain on the roof sure do take me back. Ya do look a little like yer grandmother right now, sittin' there all ears and a-wantin' to know so bad." Lizzie took a coughing spasm and spat into the coffee can. "You look like old Quanah Parker might come a-walkin' right through that back door. Ain't likely, the soldiers done kilt him. But his spirit might. Ain't no tellin'. My momma used to say, a man like that ain't got just one time

143

and place. He's liable to turn up anywhere he's called."

The rain had stopped hours ago, and birds were already chirping in the yard. It was only a little while before light began to spread over the earth and Buster crowed, waking Uncle Jerry and beginning the daily carrying of pails and the forgetting of the night.

"Ya better go on and get some sleep, sister. Ya don't look so sickly no more. 'Em stories musta done ya some good."

The fever went, and her life became something she could count on. She stood on a chair at the stove every morning, coaxing Lizzie through the making of breakfast. She went to her chickens, feeding them and tormenting them all morning. Betsy grew used to her and, when her bell was slapped, only gave the most perfunctory protest. The child wrapped her eggs carefully in Lizzie's rags and called to her aunt to put them in the cellar. Until dinner she stayed within hollering distance. Sometimes she kept Uncle Jerry company as he meandered his way through his chores. Sometimes she hummed along with Lizzie from the back step.

144

She returned to the hill next to the barn, climbing to the top and looking down at Lizzie and Uncle Jerry, almost as small as herself in the distance. She stole a watermelon and ran to the top, finding old man Cornsilk's tree and spitting the seeds far into his patch. "Don't ya shake your fist at me, old man!" she warned. She hid behind the rocks, quiet and still until she felt the air move, and then tore down the hill, her bare feet slipping from the dirt and her braids flying, the soldiers behind her, their guns pointed and horses fast. She heard the thundering behind her and saw the white settlers before her, living on Indian land, the children running and the women screaming when they heard her yell, "I am Quanah Parker!"

Just before dinner one morning, Lucie came flying down the hill, in midscream, and skidded past Lizzie. The old woman's hands were in her apron pockets and her small body stood erect. She grabbed the child's arm in flight and bent down into the little face.

"Ya be careful who ya call up. This ain't no foolishness ya can make a game of. Ya hear?" Her voice became more kindly. "I need ya to help with supper."

Lucie followed her to the chicken coop and watched as the old woman came out with a squawking bird. She took hold of the bird, carried it over to the blood-drenched stump, and pulled the hatchet from the middle of the wood. Lucie turned her back and covered her eyes.

"Sister, I want ya to watch this."

Lucie turned around but kept her hands over her eyes.

"Sister, I said for ya to watch."

Her fingers spread in a peek-a-boo. From the space between she saw the hatchet swiftly raised and thrown. Her hands shut over her eyes. She heard the bird squawk and heard the desperate flap of wings. She peeked through her fingers; the hen fluttered blindly through the yard, her headless body propelled by the need to escape, as if it were still possible to flee and save her life.

"Go on now," Lizzie said when the bird dropped. "I think ya saw enough."

After dinner an afternoon leisure crept into their lives. There was work to be done, but urgency disappeared and meditation entered. The slow repetitive care of finding and preparing food began. The heat slowed Uncle Jerry's tongue and took the edge off Lizzie's hurry, and they drifted into waiting tunes and considerations.

Lucie hung near the kitchen and garden, then found her way down the road to the creek. Some days she trailed Uncle Jerry's pole in pursuit of that smart fish, always thieving a minnow without so much as a thank you. "Your day'll come, Mister Fish," Uncle Jerry promised.

Other days her uncle didn't dare reach for his pole, and she wandered down and sat next to the creek alone. She watched for the fish, ready to run up to the house if he showed himself, and was careful of the witches, alert, as she waded near the bank, for any unfamiliar touch. Ya never knew, Uncle Jerry said, when they might be up to one a their tricks.

She tried to catch minnows in her hands, but they always dripped and wriggled through her fingers. Uncle Jerry had taught her how to crawdad, how to come up on them and snatch them into the coffee can. Even with one leg, Uncle Henry was the best crawdadder in the county. He could fill a can before most people had reached for their first one. Robert Henry and he had lived on what they could catch in the creek. If you're hungry, Aunt Lizzie said, ya learn to move real fast.

Up against the scrub trees, close to the bank, she threw gravel into the river. The circles spread and

147

spread, and she put her hand in the water to catch the circle as it came to shore. It lapped up through her hand until it reached the red earth.

"My daddy said," Uncle Jerry had told her, "this here earth lives for Indian blood. It's taken so much blood it can't git back to its natural color. He always said, this ain't no Indian Territory, it's a Indian cemetery. Course, he wasn't in his right mind near the end."

She lay back on the bank, lifting one little leg onto the other. She pulled the kerchief over her eyes. The sun was red with blue dots through the cloth. Her momma and Auney had been wrong about Uncle Jerry. He hadn't lost his mind, he just craved the sound of his own voice. And company. He was a fellow who found company in every earthly thing. He was strange, but she understood him.

She had asked him about Quanah Parker. He chuckled and shook his head. "A mean one, yessir, a real mean one." Then he had looked across the water and said quietly, "Sometimes meanness is all a man's got left."

Her leg toppled from its perch. She heard the river talking below her. She heard a merry-go-round of girls' voices, at play, at work, at home, their voices synchronized but carrying different words.

She tried to understand them, but they talked all at once, leaping and dancing further into the red and blue light until their voices became whispers. A girl in a pink dress with a red shawl stepped away from the others. As she came forward her voice became more and more defined from the rest. Lucie could see her mouth move and almost make out her words. She repeated them again and again, coming closer and closer until Lucie heard her say distinctly, "Let's go!

"Let's go," the child urged. "It's time to go."

She heard a thundering within the earth. It opened and trembled, pounding with the urgency of an assault. As it approached, she heard the striking of hooves, the dangerous gallop of horses coming very fast from a great distance. She thought they might stay on the road, but they turned up into the creek bed and pulled up before her. A dozen Indians, in Uncle Jerry's overalls and floppy hat, sat high up looking down on her. The group opened, and an Indian in a business suit with long black braids and an aquiline nose guided a large mare slowly to the front.

"Where do you come from?" he asked.

"Just up the road." She pointed in the direction of the house.

149

"What are you doing on Indian lands?"

"I'm an Indian." The Indians in overalls exchanged glances and smiled.

"Prove it," he said.

"My momma says so."

"Mothers lie, fathers lie. The Indian is a favored lie."

"My Aunt Lizzie says I am."

He guided the horse a little closer and bent close to her face. He pulled the horse back and turned around, signaling to the others to follow. Before they reached the turn in the creek, he stopped, turned to her, and called. It came to her only in echoes, circles of voices begetting other voices, begetting still more voices, and finally washing up to her.

"I am . . . I am . . . Quanah . . . Quanah . . . Parker . . . Parker."

She splashed into the creek and ran after him. "Wait," she called. She heard the howl of the wild dogs and their furious break through the trees. She ran faster in the water, her feet slick against the wet mud and the water rising. The wild dogs waited for her on both banks of the creek. In a glance she saw that one had the still-twitching headless chicken between his teeth. She ran after the horses, the dogs ran alongside the banks, and the water took more and more of her. Soon it covered her and still she ran, opening her mouth in screams of help, running, her arms raised above the water.

He pulled her up.

There were crowds on either side as the fire engine made its way down Main Street. The people roared and cheered, pushed close to the fire engine to get a look at her father. He had come home. He had reached down and pulled her onto his lap. She sat close, and he held her with one arm and waved with the other. Smiling, waving, the crowd pressed and shouted, "Quanah! Quanah! Quanah!"

From the back of the crowd J. D.'s ugly face watched the procession. Her father followed her eyes to the ugly pock-marked man, the crowd followed his eyes, and J. D. took off down an alley. The crowd pursued him, howling and yapping as they tore into him. Pieces of J. D.'s uniform flew from the alley. She heard his screams, and sirens in the distance. They came closer, yapping and tearing just behind her . . .

She was running when the fly landed on her nose. She swatted it, rubbed it, scratched it, still running, but it itched and tickled like a fur ball on her nose. She sat up and the fly buzzed away. The creek was still and the trees quiet; trouble had gone clean past her. Even the witches were asleep.

She wondered if she should tell Lizzie about her dream. Lizzie believed in dreams. She knew you were never supposed to tell your dreams until after breakfast. She knew if you dreamed of a wedding there would be a funeral, if you dreamed of a funeral there would be a wedding. One night she dreamed of a wedding dress laid out on a bed, a beautiful white wedding dress. The next night her momma came to her and said, "Lizzie, I'm a-going home. Don't ya fret." And that morning she borrowed Uncle Henry's wagon and drove up to Stilwell for her momma's funeral.

Lizzie understood the spirits in dreams. Asleep, she said, the spirits entered the body and talked in such a way as to confound a body. When Lucie had had a nightmare, Lizzie had told her to wake up and call out to the spirits, "Go on. Shoo. Scat away. Don't come bothering me with your evil talk."

"Ya have to show 'em who got the upper hand," the old woman said. Lucie had tried, trembling. Her voice wouldn't come, and the spirits laughed at her. Them wild dogs wouldn't come around bothering Lizzie, she thought.

She wondered what Lizzie would say about Quanah Parker and his pack of renegades in the creek. Would she say it was foolishness? She saw that chicken flapping around the yard looking for her head. Or maybe she'd respect her dream and say, "Sister, he done paid ya a visit." She saw herself redeemed from the antics on the hill, an extra nickel when they went into town with Uncle Henry and Aunt Bertha to sell their eggs. She heard Lizzie tell Uncle Jerry, "This here child been spoken for by Quanah Parker hisself." And Uncle Jerry, interrupting the radio announcer and saying, "I always 'spected the whole truth weren't known."

When she came out of the dirt road, she saw the Packard parked in front of the house. Somehow she wasn't surprised to see it. During the summer she had heard nothing from her mother. Uncle Henry had said she'd been down to see them, but she didn't stop by Uncle Jerry and Lizzie's place. She kicked her feet in the dirt. Her mother had come roaring down the road, like she did at Auney and Uncle Tom's, loud and ready to grab her up.

She hid behind the Packard and watched her mother and Lizzie on the porch. Lizzie was peeling potatoes, and Gracie was propped up against the porch. Uncle Jerry sat in his chair, close to the door, chewing tobacco and listening to his own voices.

Lizzie kept her eyes on her knife, now and then giving a nod from her rocker. She could hear the chatter and laughter, chatter and laughter, of her mother's high monologue. Her mother began to whine; Lizzie peeled and rocked. Her mother burst into tears; Lizzie peeled and rocked.

She had only been here for the summer, but for the rest of her life she would see her mother from Lizzie's rocker: a painted heavy face with black horizontal eyebrows and a wide red mouth, topped by yellow permed straw. A fat sloppy woman in a muumuu with a wide tear under her left armpit and a voice that either cursed or begged its way through life. As her mother grew older she settled into her body, leaving the paint and becoming partial to snap-up housedresses. But for Lucie, she was never better than the shame of that moment.

"There's my baby," her mother screamed from the porch. "Come to Momma, sweetheart. C'mon, it's your momma come back."

Gracie stood with her arms stretched open. Lucie ducked behind the Packard.

"Go on, sister," Lizzie called from the porch, "ya have to respect your momma."

She came around the car, dragging her bare feet in the dirt. She looked at her mother and waited for

154

Lizzie to say something. The old woman caught Uncle Jerry's eye and gave her rocker a deliberate swing.

"Go on," she said finally, "I don't wanna have to find me a switch to make ya behave."

Lucie stepped through the peas. Before she reached the porch, Gracie scooped her up with a whoop and left red lips on her cheeks and forehead.

"Ya been a good girl? Lizzie tells me ya loves that creek. Ya miss your momma? Ya been pining away after your momma?"

She brought her up for another kiss, and Lucie smelled the beer and cigarettes on her breath. It was worse than she remembered. Gracie offered her cheek, and the child pecked it.

"Now ain't that better? Don't ya love your momma?"

"She been a good girl." Uncle Jerry came out of his own voices to say. "Been right helpful a those chickens. Ifn ya don't count the ones died from tormenting."

Lizzie looked up from her peeling. "How'd ya say your fella died?"

"Don't no body know. When he hit the ground, he was already gone, they say. Musta been a heart attack or high blood, like Tom, Rozella's first husband."

"A body don't know when his maker gonna call him home. Ya always got to be ready for the call." Uncle Jerry considered his words. "Matty, he weren't no more'n a boy when the Good Lord took him. The last time my daddy saw 'im, his shirt was a-floating on the water. My daddy reached down to grab that shirt, but he was gone 'fore my daddy could git to 'im. We was all there at that river, and didn't none of us know a thing till we heard my daddy call out."

"He slipped on a rock trying to cross over," Lizzie said. "He weren't no more'n ten years old."

"Out of five children, there's only Henry and me left. It do make a body think."

Lucie walked over and stood beside Lizzie's rocker. They all seemed to be listening for something, and Lucie waited and watched for their words.

"Willie no more'n turned the corner . . . ," Uncle Jerry began.

Gracie laughed. "Caught with his pants down."

"I'm not saying he did right. He oughta knowed more'n to try Jewel's patience. But to take a gun and . . ."

"Don't mess with Indian women," Lizzie said. "Ain't no body meaner'n a Indian woman been crossed. He oughta knowed better'n to mess with her."

"Quanah Parker was mean." Lucie looked up at Lizzie.

"He was up to man's meanness, sister." Lizzie answered. "A woman's meanness is getting even."

"I don't reckon there's much difference 'tween the two," Uncle Jerry said. "Hate's all a same. When a person's pushed too far, it don't come specially to no man or woman."

"It seem to come more naturally to Indians," Gracie said.

Uncle Jerry chewed and considered. "Ya ain't been looking for it any place else. I reckon ya don't have to look too hard, neither. It'll find ya when it's ready."

"Old man Jeeter was a mean one," Gracie said.

"Now there's meanness, and there's meanness ain't no help to no body."

"I never did understand why my momma married 'im."

"She had two little girls and no body to look out after her. They had an understanding." Lizzie shook in a spasm, and she retched up the phlegm and spat into the coffee can. "Dear Lord. An understanding was what it was. She never did love 'im. He took on y'all and got hisself a young Indian wife."

"And she worked herself to death," Uncle Jerry said.

"I member how hard Momma worked. When she took ill, it was almost like she was happy to see that light. I member her lying on that bed. She looked peaceful as a baby. Like she was finally gitting some rest."

"My daddy was a hard man in some ways. Once Hellen took off with that Ivey man, he wouldn't let none of us have nothing to do with her."

"Henry tried to find her. But your daddy kept moving y'all round. Running from the law, we heard."

"He was no good, my daddy was right about that," Uncle Jerry said slowly. "Once we heard she was living in the Kiowa Territory, and we went down there, but they's already gone. By then he was a-going by the name a Smith."

"Did he go to jail?" Gracie asked.

"I'm not sure the law caught up with 'im." Uncle Jerry spat and wiped the brown spittle from his mouth. "But he shoulda been hung for what he did to your momma and you girls."

"He come into our settlement talking sweet things to all the young girls. Your momma didn't know better'n to listen. Robert Henry had kept her a little

158

girl, scaring all the boys away, and she didn't know better'n to fall in love with that outlaw."

"I saw Quanah Parker," Lucie said, taking her chance. "Down by the creek. He was a-riding this big horse. Came right up that creek . . ."

"I told ya, sister, ya take care who ya call up."

"Lizzie been tellin' ya 'bout her momma feeding Quanah Parker and his band a renegades?" Gracie asked with a laugh. "I heard that story many times myself. I always wandered why he took food from women and children. It don't take much a man to take the food outta the mouths a helpless women and children."

"T'weren't nothing helpless 'bout my granny. She woulda butchered all 'em animals, if he'd a needed 'em." The old woman sat her bowl of potatoes on the porch. "Indian women always had a close understanding with trouble. A body's got all she can do just keeping trouble in hand. I reckon the city's done learned ya that."

"I learned that lesson when my momma died. And we was left with old man Jeeter to use like he used his mules. Only worst."

"Didn't no body knowed where ya was at." Uncle Jerry's eyes teared; he sat straight back in his chair like a child on good behavior. "We's all sorry 'bout that. It t'weren't like the old days round Stilwell. Families was always in hollering distance. The old people was round to tell ya who ya was. Ya member old man Cornsilk, Lizzie?"

"I member." She winked at Lucie. "'Course, my memories might be a little different from yours."

"Nowadays ever body's left to do for hisself." He waited for Lizzie to stop coughing. She handed him the coffee can, and he spat in it. He seemed to forget and then remember there was people present. "Ain't nobody left 'cept me and Henry. And when we die it'll be like we never was."

"Naw, Uncle Jerry, don't say that. I always 'member you and Lizzie. Lucie here always 'member you and Lizzie. Ain't that right, sister?"

"I saw Quanah Parker. He was on a big horse right there in that creek . . ."

"You's dreamin', sister," her mother said.

"Dreams ain't so bad," Lizzie said. "Dreams can make a body powerful."

"Used to be we all had dreams. My daddy come from Georgia to git hisself some land. Sometimes I think it were his dreams made 'im so hard. Hellen were a-gonna be a fine lady and a schoolteacher. Us boys was a-gonna turn that red clay and rock into the pastures of heaven. He prayed on it something

160

turrible. He sent Hellen to pray on it. We all prayed on it ever chance we git. Seems like a man oughta knowed when to stop dreaming."

Lizzie commenced coughing. She dug her shoes into the porch and bent into her lap. Uncle Jerry held the coffee can for her.

"Maybe ya should go over to the Indian clinic." Gracie said, touching Lizzie's bent head. "They's building a lotta Indian sanitariums for the TB. In Lawton I knowed a woman cough just like that and they sent her to one of 'em sanitariums, and she come back fit as a fiddle."

"Lizzie don't wanna go."

*Lucie hears the swing of the rocker, creaking back and forth, and a low sobbing in the distance. The rustle of a breeze through the creek beds and up through the trees. The old woman steals back into bed and the child waits, quiet and still, for the old woman's arm to reach across and pull her sleeping body close.*

Lizzie straightened herself and stood up.

"Ain't no call to go to one of them places. They ain't doing nothing but help a body die. Used to be we stayed with our own kin. Now they's want a

161

herd us into pens like we's all cattle a-going to the slaughterhouse. Ya can smell it in them places. And it ain't the killing makes that powerful smell, it's the waiting and a-fearing. Well, I don't want to smell me another cow waiting and a-fearing to die. I had enough a them pens."

*I watch the old woman's face become sharper and darker as she talks. In my own time I grow into her face, my mouth turning into stubbornness, my spirit becoming still and erect, my hair growing dark and my body brown in its latent truth.*

Uncle Jerry stood up and stretched. "I sincerely wisht I knowed what went wrong. It's got so a man enjoys talking to hisself." He scratched inside his overalls. "Henry's kids got theirselves educated. They ain't got no use for our ways. You and Rozella got your own lives. The young people just go their own ways."

"Just like we done, old man."

"I ain't saying we did right. Since the old people died there don't seem to be a place for the young folk anymore." His face puzzled out his voices. "It's like we're a mess a children raising other children."

162

"The blind leading the blind," Lizzie said, pulling the screen door open. "Lord have mercy. The foolishness that's talked round here."

She winked at Lucie. "Sister, ya talk that fish outta that creek?"

"I didn't see 'im at all."

"Seeing's not the thing, sister. Ya just keep talking. 'Fore ya know it, y'all plumb tire 'im out, and he won't have no choice but to listen to ya." She held the screen door open for them. "Tomorrow's another day. Ya done that garden, old man?"

"All in the Good Lord's time."

"The Good Lord helps those helps theirselves."

The screen door swung shut, and Lucie stayed at the farm another two years. When Lizzie was taken to the sanitarium at Talihina, Gracie came roaring up the road and took her back to Lawton and Mabel's house.

One afternoon, sitting under the kitchen table, listening to her momma and Auney, she heard that Lizzie had died. Uncle Henry had passed on, and Aunt Bertha had gone to live with her youngest girl in Tulsa. Uncle Jerry had fallen on bad times. When Lizzie went to the sanitarium, he had moved back to Stilwell to be near her. He moved his pallet from family to family, living like a ghost and making bathtub beer. The last time he saw Lizzie she handed him a can full of nickels and quarters and dimes.

"My egg money," she told him. "I didn't want ya to fret 'bout burying me."

He used it to buy a television set. The county buried Lizzie in the cemetery behind the sanitarium.

"She'd turn over in her grave ifn she knowed," Gracie said.

"I believe she would."

"She was so proud a herself. Too good for Momma and the likes a us. Only one she catered to was Lucie. She tried to hang onto her, sleeping with her ever' night and telling me she was gitting better."

*In the darkness the old woman drags her coughing body to the rocker. The sobbing comes loud and distinct. Sometimes she can't move her body out of the bed, and she tries to smother her coughing sobs into the pillow. In the quiet of the night, her hold is always firm and warm, and I snuggle into its hollow. In the morning there is blood on the pillow and a bloody smear across my cheek.*

"Last time I seen her," Gracie said with the cheer of a prophet, "I knowed she was a goner. She didn't make no more sense 'n Uncle Jerry. They's like two ghosts living in their own world."

"Two ghosts," Auney said, inhaling and watching the smoke rise to the ceiling. "He ain't gonna live long 'out her."

"Ya never can tell. They say he's real happy with that television. They can't git 'im to turn the durn thing off. In his second childhood, I reckon."

Auney laughed. "Maybe it's better'n his first."

"Couldn't be no worst." her mother laughed.

"Reckon we'll git there someday, Grace?"

"Lord willing. I'm a-counting on it."

*Where have you been . . .*

WHEN THE PHONE RANG I was still prowling through my mother's house. I shifted through her closet. There was one sad housedress after another, with snaps up the front. I inspected the things on her bureau, toilet water, bobby pins, tubes of red lipstick, all covered with the sweet dust of face powder. I played with her pull-apart pearls and went through her drawers. Boxer shorts for large old ladies, ripped slips, and pinned bras, all yellow and stained with use.

It was amazing; in her seventy-two years my mother had managed to collect not one valuable thing. From the bottom of a drawer I pulled out an old composition notebook. On its cover I had written, in my perfect penmanship, *No Deposit, No Return*. The title of my first novel, inspired by the years I was known to all the local storekeepers as "the bottle girl." Those five-cent bottles had kept my mother in cigarettes and me in Pepsis and Baby Ruths, my dinner of choice. They had even, as I grew older, furnished a box or two of Kotex.

I opened the book. There, in my large careful script, my novel began:

*Eleanor Bancroft was beautiful and rich. Her skin was like the finest ivory, and her blond hair shimmered when she danced. When she danced, all the men fell in love with her. All except the handsome Nicholas Boggs. He had fallen in love with a plain, dark-haired girl from a poor family. Even though he was engaged to his little gypsy, Eleanor vowed to win him with her dancing. Someday, she hoped, someday . . .*

I turned the page, but the succeeding pages had been torn out and an envelope put in their place. "Docaments," was scrawled in my mother's hand across the front. In an afterthought, IMPORTANT was written large and underlined. Inside there was her birth certificate, Auney's birth and death (pulmonary failure) certificates, her mother's death certificate, and a burial policy for Gracie Evers from the Eternal Life Insurance Company.

I read my grandmother's death certificate. In awe and disbelief I tried to find her in the words written so casually on the form. Somewhere, some person had known her; somewhere, she had had an existence outside of women's voices.

Name: Hellen Evers Jeeter.
Husband: Leroy Jeeter.
Occupation: Wife.
Husband's Occupation: Farmer.
Date of Birth: Unknown.

169

Place of Birth: Unknown.
Name of Father: None.

*Name of Father: None. I felt my own flesh dissolve,*
*fading quickly into the never-been, never-was, vanishing*
*into the None of history. Name of Father: None. Name of*
*Mother: Not Asked.*

Cause of Death: Dust Pneumonia.

*She'd gone out to milk the cow, and when she came*
*back a light was over her shoulder. She came into the*
*house trembling and white as a ghost. "The light done*
*come for me," she said. For three nights the light came to*
*her, following her straight up to the back door. She lay*
*down in bed and told her girls, "Look for me in the moon,*
*I'll be watching ya from the moon."*

On a separate torn sheet of paper my mother had
written "Robert Henry Evers, March 26, 1897, Stilwell, Oklahoma," and, "Hellen Evers, January 16,
1932, Oaktree Cemetery, Davis, Oklahoma." The
last was the date of my grandmother's death and
place of burial, but the first date could have been
anything running across her mind at the time.

I slipped the documents and the torn sheet back

into the envelope. I flipped through the notebook and discovered my mother's hand running frantically and shamelessly through it. The sight of my mother's barely literate script always shamed me; on some level I felt she should have chosen silence. Certainly silence would have been less vulgar. But shame of her third-grade education had never kept her from writing long tortuous letters to me. The sight of those small stuffed envelopes always brought her hunger into my life. I hated them.

And her letters took patience. She demanded I decipher, understand, know when she herself did not. She tore through the common practices of spelling and punctuation, put her heart on the line for six or seven lined pages, never asked about another soul after her standard preamble, "I hope you are well," and ended abruptly with "Your Mother." It got so I could not read them, collecting them unopened on my night table until I found the courage to call her, then throwing them into the trash.

*"What do you want to be?" the preacher asked me.*
*"A writer," I said. I was six years old.*
*"A comic book writer?"*
*"No. A book writer."*

When I started writing, my mother moved from needlework to painting. What Lizzie had taken an evening to do, sitting in the parlor with Uncle Jerry and his radio, my mother had fretted over for weeks. She and Auney sat, clenching cigarettes between their teeth and talking out of the sides of their mouths, fussing a stitch through blocked designs on cotton runners. The threads were thick and gnarled and bitten, the back side a web of loops and large knots. Auney reconsidered the time it took away from her smoking and gave it up. And she watched, admiring and coaxing, as my mother fought her way through a straight border stitch.

She had no sense of color or emphasis. There was not one piece of embroidery, finished or unfinished, that did not seem hapzard, the product of random threads and needles. Her showpiece was a self-designed pillow cover that read, in hellfire red, GOD BLESS THIS HOUSE. The pillow cover fit so poorly a rubber band was wound around it to hold it in place.

But my mother was encouraged. And she moved to paint-by-numbers. She stayed within the lines, and as long as she was true to the color chart, she turned out some predictable landscapes. These she had framed and gave as birthday and Christmas gifts.

172

"I'm a-working on Rozella's painting now," she'd say when we talked. "It sure is pretty. It's got a lotta green in it."

I began writing for the local newspaper, and my mother took up the serious art of oil painting. The still life, because she could always find a bowl and some fruit or vegetables, became her favorite. They were combination pieces: the bowl was bright and large and almost recognizable, with its contents abstract and almost unidentifiable. I never ventured an opinion until I ascertained that the banana was not a squash, the apple not a tomato, and grapefruit not a cauliflower. Her masterpiece, proudly entrusted to me, was a red bowl of bananas and oranges against a chocolate brown sky. When she asked me, "Whadaya think?" I almost suggested therapy.

Her painting had no truck with dimension or nuance. She painted flat red landscapes pushed to the top of the canvas, a self-portrait of a good-looking blonde with the sly look of knowledge across her lips, and a painting of myself, looking more dead than alive in blue face and braids. Her Picasso period.

I looked around her room and wondered how she had lived with these paintings all these years. I was embarrassed by them. There was something in them, like the too-private stains in old underwear, that should be politely dressed. And I pitied her. Her desire to create, to find expression for her experience, was formidable, but when she tried to realize it away from the kitchen table, it came back stunted and deformed, a flat one-dimensional vision. Still she searched for a way to have her say and felt, especially in her paintings, that she had succeeded.

I read the title of her little manuscript in my notebook, *MY LIFE*. And my trepidation increased. I saw her, bent to her work, her hand slowly working its running scrawl, intent on the bringing and passing of her life in the written word. I was a writer, and she knew I would have to honor her words and give them a place in my own work. Blackmail. I shut the composition book and took it to the table.

I was drinking coffee and smoking one of her cigarettes when the phone rang. I walked to the phone, knowing it was Mabel and rehearsing an excuse for breakfast. The sun was barely up, and I put sleep deep into my voice.

"Miz Evers?"

"She's not here at the moment, could I take a message?"

"This is the hospital. Could you please tell her her mother passed away this morning. She went peaceful, she never did wake up."

"I'll tell her."

*"What will you do when she dies?" I ask my old friend about his troublesome mother.*

*He takes only a second, smiles, and says gleefully, "I'll blossom."*

I felt myself open to the light. I almost dropped to my knees in gratitude. I looked around the living room and considered the things I might keep. The photos of my young mother with her new baby and Lizzie and myself in front of the Packard would pack easily; everything else could just as easily be hauled away.

"What's your mother like?" new acquaintances would ask.

"She's dead."

There would be a sympathetic pause, too embarrassed to search further, and I would never have to speak of her again.

I had lived to know the end of the story. I never knew the beginning but I did know the end. I had outlived the clutch of those women's voices, and now there was only the detail of burial. I felt like running, fast and hard, as quick as the living, all the way back to California.

*"Don't mess with Indian women," I heard my mother say. And Auney's smoky laugh. "Naw, ya sure don't wanna do that."*

There is a knock on the door. I open it, and standing before me is the small Indian woman I saw at the hospital, a red shawl draped over her tiny shoulders. I smell sage burning and wait for her to speak.

"How're ya doin', sugar?"

I touch her shoulder and watch as she passes me.

Mabel comes in, full of chipper, in pedal pushers and red lips. She's carrying a plate covered with a kitchen cloth, her famous cinnamon rolls. I look around the corner of the door for the other woman and look back at Mabel.

"Ya still sleepy-eyed. Ain't you the lucky one? I don't believe I shut an eye a-worring 'bout your poor momma. I just tossed and turned, all I could do to keep from crying out loud."

"Momma's dead."

"Ya don't mean it, sugar?" She is alert, awake,

176

and already on the phone to neighbors and Lula Faye. The last few days have made her an eyewitness, a kissing kin to death, the one who lives to tell the story. I watch her face flit between opportunity and loss, tears drop, and I almost apologize for never liking her.

"I can't believe it. Only the other day, we was sitting right chere, drinking coffee and chewing the fat. Didn't have no sign atall." She is sobbing in earnest, and I should touch her and say something with comfort. But I see my mother turning the rent money can upside down on the table and watch Mabel separating her booty into piles of nickels and dimes and quarters and half dollars. I watch her hand for a quick pass over the coins. I've seen her cheat at poker.

"Will you call Johnnie?"

"Surely, sugar." She looks at me through her tears, and I know I will be featured prominently in her story. "Anything I can do to help, ya just call on me."

I walk her to the door. She slips past me, still carrying the cinnamon rolls. The smell of fresh bread and cinnamon drifts away with her.

I reach out. "Thanks for bringing the cinnamon rolls. Momma always said no one makes them like you."

"Good thing ya 'minded me. I almost forgot all 'bout 'em."

*Trash? Garbage. Refuse. The spoiled, the unusable, isolated into dumps, packed into landfills, burned in great incinerators on the edge of the city. Crap, litter, debris collected and bagged. Recycle, a mind is a terrible thing to waste. White trash: Poor, filth, human wreckage and rubbish sprawling into counties, man-made ranges of dirt and kin, inert and obscene and dangerous, bad teeth, bad skin, bad minds, bad manners aiding no expectations, a living pornography. Injun trash? Disposable, throwaway, sweepings from rotting lives and faiths, fragments of feathers and beads and paint, smut braves and squaws, the remains of a republic, the detritus of discovery.*

The rolls were gooey, a white flour mush painted with margarine and sprinkled with cinnamon and sugar. I remembered them as rare treats, a delicacy protected and craved, eaten slowly and gratefully. Now they are spongy, a crude waste of materials and calories. I pour myself another cup of coffee and lick the sugar and cinnamon from the center.

I opened my old composition book and lit another of my mother's cigarettes. *MY LIFE*, printed high and centered on the page. For a moment I was surprised by the ambition, underlined and announced. I spent my life dreaming words into place, worrying over the stories they held, and here my mother had taken up the pen as naturally as the needle or the brush. Just another craft, without a question of skill or training, never thinking of precedent or earning her art, trusting her story to win and hold her reader.

*MY LIFE.* I doubled over the table in laughter. *MY LIFE.* It was that easy, that simple to begin. I slapped the table and laughed so hard tears fell. Her long rambling letters had come just as easily. Without zip codes or correct addresses, they somehow found their way into my mailbox. I had marveled at the intuitive powers of the post office, called her attention to it, but a correct address was an incidental to her, a needless inconvenience when speaking to me.

I wiped my eyes and, shaking my head, I began reading. The preamble was expected. I realized I had been preparing for it all my life.


*Dearest Daughter,*

*I had in mine you mite need anuther storie somtimes. Its a good storie plain working people jest gitting by in*

179

*this wurld out much to be proud a cep a loving and a helping one anuther in a hard times. Corect my bad spelling an gramer I onlee went to a 3 grade I a hate fer people a knowed my ignorrence. You knowed to do it rite you got yurself edjucated not like me can't spell to save my life you knowed best.*

*I love you,*

*Your Mother*

*P.S. Rozella want to say she proud a you to she alwas knowed you a going to a be some body not like them no acounts round hear you alwas a good girl hard working like me an her yur age. Rozella say don't come back hear ain't nuthin hear but old folks and bad luck she say she love you she ben dreaming bout you when you was little.*

*I don't figure Auney a make it thru anuther winter hear she can't git her breath good an she don't go no where out her bottle of oxegin she still smoking you know Auney I sure going a miss her she ben wid me all my life I'm a glad she a going furst out me taken care a her she wouldn't a stand a chance.*

I wiped my eyes. I saw them sitting at this same table, talking it out as my mother wrote it down, Auney proud of Momma's way with words, Momma pleased with her gifts. I see Auney, off to the side in a cloud of smoke, nodding and smiling as

Momma read out her words. Even through the last words, written for me alone, Auney nodded and smiled.

When Auney died, there was no good-bye, no phone call before dawn, only a small package wrapped in yards of brown paper that found its way to my mailbox a week later. In it was a letter from my mother and a folded newspaper clipping.

*Dearest Daughter,*

*Your Auney wanted you to have this I noed you don't smoke meybe you keep it anie ways fer old time sake it still a good liter only need a little fluid good as new an reel mother of peerl to. Auney knowed she was a diein an she made me promuse not to sturb you she ditn't want a be no berden to no body you knowed how Auney is. Im reel glad I payd her insurence all these years she had a reel nice berin I got a sutharn bapist preecher an we all singin Amasin Grace I knowed Auney was talken to me. I want to go jest the same way reel nice.*

*I love you,*
*Your Mother*

I kept that lighter in my tweed jacket for years, bringing Auney into classrooms and meetings, touching the handle as I spoke of Dickens and Eliot

181

and Arnold's distant shore. The jacket went out of fashion, and I changed to solid wools.

The newspaper clipping was an expected enclosure. Along with her artistic commitments, my mother took to reading the paper in her later years, collecting clippings on themes relevant, she thought, to particular times of my life. When I went away to college there came a weekly dispatch of rapes and murders of young girls, on mothers' sacrifices to give their children better lives, on mothers who had lost their children. When I was married there came articles on recognizing a bad marriage, how to get out of a bad marriage ("50 Ways to Leave Your Lover," one was titled), how to file for a divorce without a lawyer. When she retired from the cafeteria and began living on Social Security, there came feature articles on poverty in old age, sex after seventy, Gray Panther rallies, and again, her perennial theme, rapes and murders of women living alone.

But this clipping was different. They always arrived without comment, sometimes without accompanying letters, trusting me to decipher, to understand, to know why she had taken a scissors and carefully cut this article from the paper, addressed an envelope, and sent it to me. Sometimes,

I was just plain dumbfounded or too embarrassed to mention it to her.

This headline ran across a full page, MOTHER OF FIVE LEAVES HUSBAND AND CHILDREN FOR ALASKA. It was the early seventies, in the first struggle of feminism, and such articles about the shocking and unnatural behavior of women was not uncommon. After reading it, my eye caught the tiny scrawl high in the right-hand corner, *I wished I was this woman*.

Until that moment I had never guessed the burden of Auney on my mother. She had raised two daughters, raising children since she was a child herself.

"Ya take good care a your sister," her mother had said on her dying bed, and the girl had stepped into motherhood at nine years old.

I returned to the composition book. There was a space of several lines after the preamble, and then "My Life," printed and centered once again, announced the story to come. I read quickly through the ten or twelve pages, and I knew they were written without Auney's encouragement or knowledge. They were written alone, perhaps with Auney asleep on the couch or in the grave, but written in a single rushed and hurt voice. They were not the stories I had heard at the kitchen table. These were the details of a girl child growing up abandoned and unprotected, silenced in beer and laughter; these were the stories that spun the others, making the laughter high and loud, building a hysteria of family and need, holding without splitting and running without distance.

I closed the book and sat, staring through the plastic cover on the couch, waiting to decipher, to understand, to know what she had wanted me to know. I wondered if the plush of the red velvet ran in the same flat direction all over the couch, or if there were areas, here and there, not smooth with age.

*"You do the right thing," my mother wrote.*

*"Do right," Auney said.*

*"Don't wash your dirty linen in public," Lizzie warned. "Ever' story ain't for repeating. A body don't need to tell ever thing he knowed."*

I picked the book up and walked into the kitchen. There were things to do, a preacher to see, a song to be sung, and a life taken back. I put the book in the sink, struck a kitchen match, and lit the page of my novel first. I watched the story blacken and disintegrate into flakes of ash. I lit the the last

184

pages of my mother's story and watched as the last pages consumed the middle and the beginning. The cardboard cover smoked and then leaped into fire, rising high into my face, and leaving only a sink full of ashes.

I did not hate her then.

The undertaker remembered my mother from her arrangements with Auney. He knew a Southern Baptist preacher and his staff could sing "Amazing Grace." He took a drag on his cigarette, looked through a file, and said, "I know somebody who does a nice Cherokee chant. With drums?"

"A chant?"

"I see your momma said her momma was a full-blooded Cherokee."

"Who knows?"

He leaned across his desk, almost whispering. "My own grandmomma was Choctaw."

"Oh. What did my mother say?"

"She said she wouldn't know Cherokee if she heard it."

"I'm with her."

*The Lord is my shepherd; I shall not want. He maketh me to lie down in green pastures: he leadeth me beside the*

*still waters. He restoreth my soul: he leadeth me in the
paths of righteousness for his name's sake. Yea, though I
walk through the valley of the shadow of death, I will fear
no evil . . .*

Mabel and Lula Faye stood next to me as the casket was lowered into the ground. There were a few people around the grave, neighbors, bingo buddies, and Johnnie Bevis hung on the edge. He was in his seventies, still carrying a roughness from his forty years in the oil fields. The day before he had shown up at the house asking to pick up his things. He tiptoed from room to room, acknowledging me with a shake of his head and saying, "Your momma sure was a good woman." When the preacher finished reading, I saw him shake his head and move toward me, his lips moving.

"Thank you for coming, Johnnie." I shook his hand and turned to find Mabel's car.

*Then I saw her. A doe came out of the trees on the hill.
She fixed me with her eyes and waited. The mourners
shook my hand and from a distance I heard their comfort-
ing words. We stood, the two of us, each watching the
other. A stillness surrounded her, no leaf fluttered and no
bird sang, the earth paused, waiting as I waited, giving*

186

*up this moment to her peace. She came a little closer, stared at me and spoke, some untranslatable language known only to the spirit and her stillness entered my blood.*

*From behind the trees another doe appeared and another, a dark-eyed beauty with her small fawn. They came to the side of the doe and stood, unafraid and watchful, interested observers, protected in her stillness. Only the fawn skittered and leaped behind the trees. The other three remained. I heard Mabel directing me home.*

I canceled my classes in California and stayed in my mother's house a week. I agreed to leave the furniture in the house, and Mabel, happy in her furnished rental, trooped through the house with prospective tenants. I slept on the pallet and ate at the Chicken Shack, moving slowly through the days and falling into a determined sweaty sleep. In a store window I caught a glimpse of the small Indian woman, and I eased forward to catch her, with the stealth of a cat, pushing my face into my own reflection.

I woke in the early mornings to watch the moon and wait for the sun, restless in the silence around me. I drank coffee and smoked cigarettes and said, "Ain't nothing like a cigarette and coffee in the morning," and stared into the resting darkness around me. The day grew light, the traffic grew louder, and I returned to my pallet.

I cannot look at the moon without searching it for mothers, known and unknown. I still get up before dawn and wait for the whispering of secrets. I listen for them stealing toward me in some grand conspiracy, carrying my story within them, a child of lives passed in trust, a bride to the confidences of women. And I have been faithful, straying only for another confidence, another voice whispering its secrets urgently to me and willing me with every word into honor and faith.

*Nu la*

*. . . hurry*

SEVERAL YEARS after my mother's death I returned to Oklahoma City to file an amended death certificate for my grandmother. I had written many letters protesting the unknowns and the cancellation of my grandmother's father in *None*. Their policy demanded documents. Oral histories were not reliable sources, they insisted, and so I found myself in the Oklahoma Historical Society room, looking for proof that my grandmother had had a father. Around me sat comfortable retirees, ready at last to discover their Indian heritage. They were ardent and organized, researchers in their old age, with manila folders and sharp No. 2 pencils.

I had come with no folders or pencils, believing my presence sufficient to the pursuit. Patiently, I waited my turn at the Cherokee rolls. For over an hour I waited, then heard my name called.

Evers . . . Lucie.

I went up to the librarian's desk, anxious to get a look at this book that kept everyone so busy. The reverence of researchers had touched me, and I moved toward the desk with careful Sunday steps.

"Lucie Evers," I said.

The librarian was a pink middle-aged man. From his sitting position I could see the balding circle at the top of his head. He looked up and grinned.

"Who do you think you are?" he said.

"Lucie Evers."

"No," he sighed, "what tribe?"

"Cherokee?" I said, but heard the question in my voice.

He smirked and reached behind him for the book. He stretched the heavy black book toward me, grinning broadly at the joke.

*Cherokee Rolls, Dawes Commission.*

I move forward and stretch out my hand, but I cannot take the book. My face burns, and I cannot look up. I know this anger. I've seen it on the faces of Lizzie, Auney, and Momma, it has even flashed across Uncle Jerry's simple face. And, once, I've known it to leap into me, quick and dangerous, reckless in size and circumstance and consequence.

I watch myself reach down and take hold of his collar. My hands curl around the cotton and the top button flies. I pull him across the desk into my face. I speak slowly, deliberately, beyond the rush of anger, blood talking low and clear.

"I ain't asking you to tell me who I *think* I am. I am the great-granddaughter of Robert Henry Evers, I am the granddaughter of Hellen Evers Jeeters, I am the daughter of Gracie Evers, the niece of Rozella Evers, and the grandniece of Lizzie Sixkiller Evers."

My hands almost relax, but I catch the grin forming at the corners of his pale thin mouth.

"Let me put it to you this way. I am a follower of stories, a negotiator of histories, a wild dog of many lives. I am Quanah Parker swooping down from the hills into your bedroom in the middle of the night. And I am centuries of Indian women who lost their husbands, their children, their minds so you could sit there and grin your shit-eating grin."

I eased him back against his chair and took a pen from my pocket.

I said, waving the pen, "I am your worst nightmare: I am an Indian with a pen."

I took the Cherokee book and headed back to my place at the table. The scene had not taken the retirees away from their folders or pencils. When I left, I returned the book to him and scratched my name off the list. He kept his face so still I had to laugh.

"Look," I said. "It's nothing personal. I've just had one too many white men in my life."

I smiled and he tried to raise the corners of his mouth.

"I'm going to give you some advice, passed on to me by the old people." I have his attention. He leans toward my words.

"Don't mess with Indian women," I say. He's still waiting, confused. "That's all. You don't need to know no more than that."

I walk through the door into the corridor and up the stairs. I hear steps above and below, small quick steps, moving with the force and lightness of ghosts. Women's voices crowd around me, remembering and clucking and giggling over his scared pink face.

"Don't mess with Indian women," the voices whoop.

And I hear Auney say, slow and pleased, "Naw, I sure wouldn't wanna do that."